villainet

ANDY BRIGGS
VILL@IN.NET

Council
of
Evil

Walker & Company New York

First published in Great Britain in 2008 by Oxford University Press
Published in the United States of America in 2009 by Walker Publishing Company, Inc.
Visit Walker & Company's Web site at www.walkeryoungreaders.com

For information about permission to reproduce selections from this book, write to
Permissions, Walker & Company, 175 Fifth Avenue, New York, New York 10010

Library of Congress Cataloging-in-Publication Data
Briggs, Andy.
Council of evil / Andy Briggs.
p.   cm.   — (Villain.net)
Summary: Fourteen-year-old Jake Hunter goes from average bully to villain after finding
a Web site that lets him download superpowers, but when he joins forces with the
supervillain Basilisk, he may be in over his head.
ISBN-13: 978-0-8027-9517-5 • ISBN-10: 0-8027-9517-X
[1. Bullies—Fiction. 2. Good and evil—Fiction. 3. Superheroes—Fiction.] I. Title.
PZ7.B76528Co 2009   [Fic]—dc22   2008040639

Printed in the U.S.A. by Quebecor World Fairfield
2 4 6 8 10 9 7 5 3 1

All papers used by Walker & Company are natural, recyclable products made
from wood grown in well-managed forests. The manufacturing processes conform to
the environmental regulations of the country of origin.

VILLAIN.NET is used in this work as a fictitious domain name. Walker & Company
and OUP take no responsibility for any actual Web site bearing this name.

For Mum
Always being there . . .

From: Andy Briggs
To: VILLAIN.NET readers everywhere
Subject: Careful on the Web!

As you know, the Internet is a brilliant invention, but you need to be careful when using it in your plans for world domination . . . or just doing homework.

In this book, the villains (and heroes!) stumble across the different Web sites accidentally. But VILLAIN.NET and HERO.COM don't really exist. :-(I thought them up when I was dreaming about how cool laser vision would be. The idea for VILLAIN.NET suddenly came to me—especially the scene when Jake shoots the . . . Oh, wait! You haven't read it yet, so I'd better not spoil it! :-) Anyway, I began writing and before I knew it, the idea had spiraled into HERO.COM as well. But I had made up all of the Internet stuff. None of it is really out there on the Web, unfortunately.

Here are my cool tips for safe surfing on the Web: keep your identity secret (like all heroes do); stick to safe Web sites; make sure a parent, teacher, or guardian knows that you're online; don't bully anyone else—that's seriously not good—and if anyone ever sends you anything that makes you feel uncomfortable, don't reply, and tell an adult you trust.

I do have my own Web site, and it's totally safe: **www.heroorvillainbooks.com**

Be safe out there!

:-)

CONTENTS

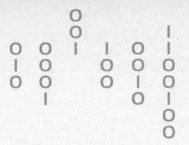

Storming the Beach

The assault force emerged from the ocean as silent as ghosts.

Jake Hunter watched them from his craggy vantage point. With the distinctive crunch of leather, Jake clenched his gloved fist. His confusion and anger seemed to enhance his superpowers. And after all the betrayal, lying, and violence that had surrounded him recently, the powers felt stronger than ever. It felt as though pins were stabbing his fingertips.

"Darn it . . . there go my gloves," he muttered under his breath as his fingernails extended like cats' claws, thickening as they ripped through the tips of his gloves. They formed long, razor-sharp talons that shone like black marble in the moonlight.

A week ago he had been just an ordinary kid. Now he was a superpowered global fugitive wanted for theft, kidnapping, blackmail; and he was instrumental in the pending destruction of the planet.

Not bad for a fourteen-year-old.

The spear of rock he was standing on poked out of

the surrounding jungle and allowed him to see across the island. It was bathed in the silver light of a full moon, which highlighted the white-sand beach. It could almost be paradise—if not for the fact that Jake's actions had cost him *everything*: his family, friends, and security.

Cost him his whole life.

Knowing that it was all his own fault did not lessen the anger he felt inside. Anger was the only thing keeping him going right now.

The line of black amphibious Sea Crawlers that emerged from the ocean spoiled the view for him. The Crawlers were the size of buses and rode on a set of caterpillar tracks like tanks. Once they had safely landed ashore, hydraulic ramps powered down at the rear of each vehicle and soldiers emerged in military formation. Jake could just distinguish that they were all armed with rifles and wearing bulky combat jackets as they raced toward the tree line.

They were Enforcers—an elite force of soldiers created by the United Nations specifically to control super-powered misfits such as Jake.

"They must be warm with all that gear on," thought Jake. He was sweating profusely and wiped beads of sweat from his brow, taking care not to poke his eye out with his lethal talons. The tropical heat was relentless, even at night. His black jeans clung to his legs. Worse still, they rode up his backside but he couldn't pull them loose for fear of slicing himself with his claws.

Jake rose into the air. It felt just like rapidly ascending in an elevator. He focused his mind, realizing that he was going to need a lot of firepower if he was going to take out the invading party. His fingers stretched painfully apart as an invisible power swelled in his palms. He closed his eyes and it felt as though he was holding a pair of bowling balls at arm's length. When he flicked his eyes back open, they burned like fiery coals. His vision was bathed in red, enhancing living creatures from the general background clutter by showing the electrical pulses through their bodies. He now saw them as shimmering figures, almost like angels. There was nowhere for them to hide.

Jake tilted forward and was suddenly rocketing over the palm trees. Within thirty seconds he was at the beach before any of the advancing army could reach cover.

To the men on the ground it looked as if a huge black vulture was descending on them. They all raised their rifles to fire as he swooped overhead, arms extended toward the ground.

Jake felt twin cones of force erupt from his hands and punch into the Enforcers. Some of the men were hurled through the air. The troopers left standing had the presence of mind to squeeze their triggers and shoot.

Most of the bullets missed Jake and combed through the air in the wake of his flight path. But some of the Enforcers remembered enough from their training to "lead" the target—shooting *ahead* of Jake's trajectory. These bullets struck him.

To Jake, the impact of the bullets felt like he was being tickled. They struck an invisible shield inches from his body—and the air sparkled with fine blue crackles as his translucent force field absorbed them.

Jake brought himself upright, hovering just a few feet off the ground, and spun around, firing another cone of energy. To anybody watching, the cone looked like the heat haze that danced above the surface of a road on a hot day. His blast hit one of the Sea Crawlers just as the last Enforcer jumped out. The Crawler buckled like a can and flipped sidelong, rolling a dozen times across the sand before splashing into the water.

Jake shot up vertically as another volley of gunfire shredded the palm trees behind him. The soldiers took the opportunity to sprint for their lives across the beach, dragging fallen comrades to their feet and into the shelter offered by the trees.

Jake was so high up that he was beyond the range of the weapons. He paused to take in the impressive view of the island, which sprawled around the smoldering opening of a gigantic volcano.

He stared beyond his feet, and far below he could

easily see the electric outlines of the troops who thought they were safely concealed in the jungle. He let out a heavy sigh, knowing he had better finish this.

Jake dived straight down, arms outstretched, and willed another burst of energy from his hands. It zeroed straight for the second Sea Crawler.

The Enforcers cowering in the trees watched as an invisible hammer smashed the Crawler's cab three feet under the sand—the tail of the vehicle was left poking at an angle into the air.

"Sarge!" wailed a terrified young soldier.

"Pipe down!" growled a muscular sergeant with a British accent.

Jake landed with a thump on the beach, facing the men. He allowed his long claws to tap rhythmically against his leg, in what he hoped was a menacing manner. His clothes absorbed the moonlight, and his glowing eyes gave him a fearsome appearance.

"Um . . . yeah . . . ," he mumbled. He couldn't think of *anything* suitably threatening to say. His head was still swimming with recent revelations.

Then the ground shook, making every bone in his body vibrate and his teeth rattle. The braver of the troopers risked a glance behind, through the foliage, at the volcano. A massive plume of smoke spewed from the volcano's cone, lit by flaming debris.

It had begun.

Jake's actions over the last week had been truly awful, even by his own standards. But they were nothing compared to the erupting volcano and what it signified. Jake knew that the Core Probe had been launched and was now burrowing to the center of the earth.

After the backstabbing treachery of the past few days, it looked as if he'd either be dead or in a cell on Diablo Island before he learned the consequences of his actions.

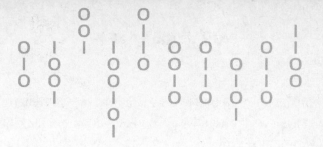

Spam

The alarm clock's beep was unceremoniously loud, forcing Jake's eyes open from a dreamless sleep. His hand snaked out and thumped the clock silent, but it had started a chain reaction that would ultimately lead to school.

His mother's muffled voice yelled from the kitchen. "Jacob! Time to get up! Come get some breakfast."

The rest of his family was already up. His mother was eating a bowl of cereal as she peered through her glasses at the newspaper, while his father watched a small television set on the counter, running a twenty-four-hour news program. His sister, Beth, was in the crisp blue uniform of her private girls' school, reading a letter. She waved it at him as he stumbled downstairs.

"From my pen pal in New Zealand!" she said excitedly.

"What, is she too poor to have e-mail?" That wiped the stupid grin from her smug face. Beth scowled at him, then turned back to her letter.

"Toast?" his father asked as he loosened his too-tight tie.

"Nah," muttered Jake as he slumped into his chair.

"Sleep well?" asked his mother without taking her eyes from the paper.

Jake shrugged, and an affirmative "Mmm" rumbled from the back of his throat. He'd found this method of answering almost any question usually stopped his parents from asking anything else. Sure enough, his mother nodded and continued reading. Jake disliked these family moments together, but, try as he might, he couldn't blame his parents. They worked hard, provided a comfortable home, were never short of money, and allowed their children to have a huge amount of independence. But somehow Jake had never felt comfortable. While the independence had made his sister a nerdy brain, Jake had gone down a different track—and he was beginning to regret it.

On his walk to school, girls threw him flirting, shy glances. He was a good-looking boy, with short, spiky blond hair. Even the school office secretary tended to be extra nice no matter how often he was sent to the principal's office.

Boys, on the other hand, usually gave him a wide berth, and an appraising look. Jake Hunter was the school's most formidable bully—not somebody to cross. But there was a vague aura of respect from his fellow classmates for the way he manipulated the adults, and on several occasions had defended students from being picked on by rival schoolkids infiltrating their territory.

But Jake was unaware of this side of his reputation. The other boys' actions made him feel both angry and lonely. Not an emotion he'd share with anyone, of course. He'd always stood up for himself, and this had naturally seemed to lead into bullying others. Now "bully" was a tag he was forced to wear, a preemptive act that actually prevented *him* from being bullied by the more unscrupulous characters in school.

Those losers had become his friends.

He made it most of the way to school alone before he ran into his crew. They might be his friends, but he didn't really trust any of them, and he knew the feeling was mutual.

Anthony Culkin, or Big Tony, was huge. He claimed he had big bones, but even as Jake approached, Big Tony was already polishing off his packed lunch.

"Hunter!" he said by way of greeting, chunks of half-chewed sandwich falling from his mouth. The others turned to acknowledge their unofficial leader.

Knuckles, aka Raymond Olson, was a little taller than Jake, and much stronger. His face was pale and greasy, and his small squinting eyes made him resemble some kind of rodent. He flicked his head to one side, then the other, like he'd seen boxers do before a fight. The result was a hideous crack from somewhere in his neck. Jake was sure that wasn't healthy, but he tried not to react.

Scuffer was a small kid, who made up for his stature with a bad attitude. Warren Feddle was his real name, and he took time to punch anyone who dared to use it. Scuffer was the worst of the bunch. He had a real criminal mind and enjoyed inflicting pain.

Jake never did that. He beat up some of the kids who irritated him, but it wasn't *personal*. Jake merely saw it as the order of things, a food chain with the cunning predators at the top and the dumber animals underneath. But Scuffer, he was a nasty piece of work. *Everything* he did was personal.

"Look! It's the Professor!" Scuffer yelled with delight. They all followed his pointing finger. Sure enough the lone figure of the "Professor" was slouching as he walked to school, looking as miserable as Jake felt. His back was to them, and he hadn't sensed the sudden danger he was in.

"Let's grab his backpack!" Knuckles suggested with his irritating shrill voice that didn't fit his muscular frame.

And do what with it? thought Jake. But already the gang was charging recklessly across the street, yelling at the top of their lungs:

"Hey! Professor!"

"Gonna pound you, geek!"

The kid turned, looking terrified, and fled as fast as

he could. Jake dimly remembered his name was Pete. He was as harmless as a fly; but then again, flies never punched back.

Despite himself, Jake cheered up a little and beamed as he joined in the pursuit. "The thrill of the chase," he thought.

During classes Jake entertained himself by flicking pieces of soggy chewed paper at his victims across the class. The teachers shot him suspicious glances, but remaining undetected was an art form Jake had perfected over the years.

Jake and his gang prowled the yards at lunchtime, like sharks through a reef. But today people were avoiding them successfully, and there wasn't much fun to be had. So they ended up kicking a soccer ball around on an empty field. Of course, one of the teachers took exception to this innocuous activity and yelled at them to get off the field.

"Typical," thought Jake. Do something harmless and they get shouted at, but when they were deliberately starting a fight they always got away with it. That proved to Jake that justice was more of a concept than a reality.

One of the few classes that Jake and Scuffer were actually in together was computer class. Jake sneakily surfed the Internet, glancing at the Web site of his favorite rock band: Ironfist. He had been scrolling through the message board, where some fans were heaping praise on their new release, when Scuffer leaned over and tugged his sleeve.

"Look at this," he whispered conspiratorially. He held up a USB memory stick.

"What is it?" said Jake.

"My uncle's computer got a virus. It's so new his virus software didn't pick it up. It trashed everythin' he had, all his documents, music, and photos. All gone. 'Cept he didn't realize that when he'd tried to back up his stuff, he copied the virus onto this. Wanna see what happens when we stick it into the school's network?"

Despite himself, Jake laughed out loud. The teacher threw a glance his way but was too involved in helping another student with a problem on her screen. Crashing the school network would be a terrible offense; and therefore carry great bragging rights if they could get away with it.

"Sure, go ahead."

"Put it on your computer," Scuffer said, forcing the memory stick into Jake's hand.

"No way! If they trace it to me I'll get expelled!"

"So?"

Jake knew he would never hear the end of that from his parents. He glanced at the boy next to him, who was staring between a problem sheet and his answer on the screen. Jake didn't pause for thought. He reached out and scrunched the boy's question sheet into a ball, then threw it across the room. The boy looked at him with a mixture of fear and astonishment. He hesitated, then without breathing a word, climbed from his chair to retrieve his discarded sheet.

The moment the boy's back was turned Jake thumbed the USB drive into the computer port. He gave it a few seconds and hoped the virus was copying itself, before yanking it out just as the boy picked up the paper and spun back around, apprehensively returning to his seat.

Jake and Scuffer swapped grins, then looked enthusiastically at their own screens. From the corner of his eye, Jake saw the boy was straightening out his answer sheet, unaware that the virus was infiltrating his machine. Jake decided to check his e-mails as he waited.

The boy frowned when he looked at his screen, where a spinning hourglass had replaced the cursor, indicating his computer was busy. He experimentally jiggled the mouse. Nothing happened.

Jake typed in his password and accessed his e-mail. He had a few pieces from the Ironfist Web site, and one from Big Tony: a photo of a chimp riding a motorcycle. Jake shook his head; Big Tony was always forwarding junk to people on the assumption that if *he* found it funny, *they* would too.

"Miss Campbell," the boy said in a timid voice.

Jake glanced at the boy's screen: the computer pointer was moving across the screen unaided, opening any file or folder it came across. This resulted in a mass opening of programs, all executing in a torrent of separate windows that flooded the screen. It was as though an angry poltergeist had taken over.

Jake hid his delight and checked another e-mail. This one was peculiar; the sender's name was the same as his own. The name "JAKE HUNTER" burned on the screen with the subject message:

"JAKE, JOIN ME AND RULE!"

He moved the mouse across.

"Miss Campbell!" screamed the boy so loudly that everybody turned to look at him. "I think my computer's got a virus!" His screen was thick with windows opening so fast that it flickered.

"Daniel, what have you done?" began Miss Campbell.

"ALL DATA ERASING" suddenly appeared on the boy's screen in letters big enough for the whole class to see.

"No!" he yelped as the computer screens on either side of him turned deep blue, and a mass of computer code raced across them. The Internet browser disappeared as Jake was about to click on the mysterious e-mail.

Computers began to crash like dominoes around

the classroom, leaving a wake of complaints from surprised students.

"Turn them off! Turn them off!" yelled their teacher, but it was too late—the virus had spread in a spectacular manner through the school network and onto the servers, where it would be particularly destructive.

Jake felt a flurry of activity behind him and braced himself for the reprimanding hand of Miss Campbell on his shoulder.

"What have you done?" she cried.

Jake looked up, relieved to see that Miss Campbell was towering over the boy next to him. The boy's face was a picture of shock, something that made Jake smile all the way home.

Jake managed to avoid spending too much time with his gang after school; he just wasn't in the mood to be standing around on a street corner as it got dark. He'd left them outside Patel's newsstand with the shopkeeper loudly complaining that they should hang out somewhere else.

Jake just wanted to head home. Lately he'd felt *something* was missing from his life. Everything he did seemed a little too predictable and boring. He was smart enough to know that only *he* had the power to change that.

Loud Ironfist tracks pumped from his computer

speakers, and with any luck the blaring music would bother his sister. Jake pulled up his e-mail and saw he had one unread message. He clicked on it.

FROM: Jake Hunter

TO: Jake Hunter

SUBJECT: Jake, join me and rule!

The sender's e-mail address was different from his own; in fact, following the swirling @ sign was a jumble of characters that seemed assembled from dozens of world alphabets. It was complete nonsense, probably just spam: junk e-mail. But with nothing else to do Jake sighed and clicked on it anyway.

The e-mail opened up in a separate window that drifted through several different languages before settling into English.

"Jake Hunter, unleash your true potential and click here to join me at VILLAIN.NET—the world awaits you!"

Jake hesitated, the mouse pointer hovering over the link. "Why bother?" he thought. As if in answer to the unspoken question the text shifted on the screen. Jake read it in surprise.

"Because you feel you need something *more*. I offer you the power to rule the world with a simple mouse click. Join me, Jake Hunter. It's in your blood."

Jake frowned. Somebody had gone to a lot of trouble to make it stand out from the usual spam he got. Then a thought occurred to him: "This must be just another of Big Tony's stupid e-mails."

The screen suddenly went black.

Jake felt a moment's dread and hoped he hadn't just infected his own computer. The screen changed to a blinding white that hurt his eyes before slowly fading to reveal a plain-looking Web site. A banner declared:

"VILLAIN.NET—WELCOME!"

Underneath was a single animated icon. Jake clicked on it, waiting for something stupid to appear. Several new icons appeared below a message.

"You have been selected to receive a free gift that will allow you to conquer the world." As long as the gift involved shooting something, then he wouldn't complain. A game would help him relieve the boredom. He continued to read. "You will be granted a single temporary power for demonstration purposes. After you have demonstrated your ability you will be met by one of our representatives. Click below."

Jake glanced through the range of icons on offer. Some were stick figures with various lines and shapes emanating from them, others were just shapes and logos. One particular logo seemed familiar, but he couldn't quite place it. He clicked on it.

The screen rippled as though made from liquid and he could have sworn it warped into a slender finger that tapped him gently on the forehead. The whole

experience was over in a second, leaving Jake a little dizzy and doubting anything had actually happened. He certainly didn't feel any different, and when he looked back at the screen, the Web site had vanished.

"Stupid site," muttered Jake. He must be more tired than he thought. With resignation, he cranked up the music, turned his attention to his TV at the foot of his bed, and started up his Xbox console. Within a minute he was lost in a world of rampaging monsters. Midway through the game he noticed a symbol on a door within the game's environment. It was the same as the one he'd clicked on earlier and now he recognized it.

It was a radiation-warning symbol.

Jake awoke with a surprising spring in his step. He met his gang and thoroughly enjoyed chasing the Professor; delivering a wedgie to him that was so severe they could hear his boxers rip. Leaving the geek on the floor, writhing in agony, the bullies strolled into school.

Jake nonchalantly asked Big Tony what the Web site link was supposed to be, but Tony had such a blank expression that Jake assumed he must have already forgotten that he'd sent it.

Maybe it was because he was feeling unusually cheerful that the day was passing quickly, and at lunch he noticed a pretty girl with long brown hair smiling at him.

Spam

Jake felt a little embarrassed and was thankful he wasn't with his gang. He had seen her a few times before and knew her name was Lorna, but he had never summoned up the courage to speak to her.

Now he found they were walking in the same direction.

"Hi, Jake."

"Hi," he mumbled, staring at his feet.

"What are you doing over the break? Any plans?"

Jake felt his mouth become dry and had a sudden attack of nerves as she looked at him with deep brown eyes. "I . . . um . . . nothing. Usual stuff, probably. You?"

Lorna shifted nervously but didn't stop smiling. "Same. Nothing new."

They stopped outside the art room, Jake's destination. They looked at each other in silence for an uncomfortably long time, lost for idle conversation. Then Jake noticed three kids, a couple of years his junior, were picking on a boy who was clearly cornered and outnumbered. Seeing an opportunity to break the silence and act the hero, Jake intervened. The three bullies made a quick escape, thinking that Jake was protecting his standing as school thug—while their victim stared wide-eyed, thinking Jake wanted the honor of beating him up instead.

"Hunter!" screamed Mr. Falconer, the art teacher, as he rushed from the classroom. "Stop that right now!"

Jake looked confused. The bell suddenly rang and a

friend of Lorna's came up and pulled her toward her classroom and out of sight. Mr. Falconer was upon him, bristling with rage.

"I saw what you did!" rumbled the teacher, obviously misunderstanding.

Jake frowned and looked around for the boy he had saved, but the kid had vanished into the mass of students filing into their classes.

"What're you talking about? I was helping that—"

"You can explain yourself in detention!" snarled Mr. Falconer.

The last place anybody wanted to be on a Friday, just before winter break, was in detention. That included the teachers and it made Mr. Falconer's temper all the more heated.

"This is unacceptable behavior, Hunter," he snapped as he paced back and forth.

"I told you, I was stopping that kid from being beaten up!"

"A likely story. Save your lies!" Mr. Falconer's finger quivered with rage. "I know your type, Hunter. I had to put up with them myself when I was a boy. Picking on younger kids; you should be ashamed of yourself!"

Jake was so angry at the injustice of it all. He started to feel a burning pain in his gut like very bad indigestion and he beccame uncomfortably warm. The words slipped from his mouth before he could stop them. "Are you stupid? Or does that egghead of yours make you deaf?"

Falconer went apoplectic. "That's it! I'm going to make sure you have detention for the rest of the year—"

But Jake wasn't listening. He'd zoned out and was looking around with a frown. "Do you smell that?"

"I'm talking to you, Hunter! Don't ignore me!"

"It smells like burning wood."

Mr. Falconer opened his mouth to argue back, but stopped as the distinctive odor caught his nostrils. It was getting stronger by the second. They both scanned the room with growing concern before spotting fine white smoke curling from the planks of wood stacked against one wall.

"Fire!" yelled the teacher rather pointlessly.

Before he could move toward the fire alarm, the workbench in front of him was suddenly ablaze. An orange tongue of flame punched toward the ceiling and caught the tiles. Mr. Falconer backpedaled in astonishment as all the other wooden workbenches were engulfed by the inferno.

Jake looked around frantically. Even the window frames had started to smolder, and a small potted plant on the corner of the teacher's desk was now aflame.

Jake knew he should move, but something bizarre caught his attention.

His hands and arms were glowing with a green energy that randomly shot out from his body and set fire to whatever it touched. Luckily, Mr. Falconer was turned the other way, running toward a fire extinguisher.

Streamers of green energy lashed from Jake's body, and he watched in amazement as they struck the steel legs of the stools around the room and buckled them as if they'd suddenly turned to rubber.

Mr. Falconer stretched for the fire extinguisher on the wall but pulled his hand away from the invisible wave of heat radiating from the cylinder. Another streamer caught the metal tank and it began to melt like wax. The pressurized contents exploded outward, metal fragments embedding in the burning benches next to Jake and the teacher.

More ceiling tiles ignited with a loud *WHUMP*, and the flames rapidly spread above them, dripping burning debris down.

"Hunter! Get—" Mr. Falconer stopped in surprise. He saw Jake's entire body was glowing with a green aura that extended several inches from his body. Even as he watched, Mr. Falconer could feel his mustache start to singe. He batted at it and looked around in panic for an escape route, but the room was now thick with smoke.

A distant fire alarm was triggered, but that was

drowned out by an earth-shattering crack as lumps of the flaming ceiling started to drop. A chunk of plaster struck Mr. Falconer's head, and he fell unconscious to the floor.

Jake's anger had been replaced by fear and he ran for the door, fueled by an instinct for self-preservation. He glanced at his hands—the weird glow had vanished. He hesitated at the exit.

The room was now a cauldron of fire, but strangely, Jake didn't feel the heat at all. He looked down at the prone body of his teacher, who moments before didn't have the time of day to listen to reason. Now the flames were approaching him with each passing second.

Jake hesitated. He knew he should go back inside and drag his teacher out, but the room was blazing and he doubted that anyone could survive a rescue mission.

And whatever power had erupted from him now seemed to have faded away, so there was no certainty he would survive either.

Precious seconds ticked by as Jake hesitated. . . .

A Meeting in the Dark

Clouds of steam billowed from the remains of the art room as the fire crews bathed it with high-pressure hoses. The seasoned firefighters marveled at the ferocity of this outburst; they had rarely seen anything that could melt metal the way this conflagration had.

Jake was sitting on the bumper of an ambulance looking, and feeling, completely fine. He didn't even have signs of smoke inhalation. He had eventually doubled back and dragged Mr. Falconer from the inferno. Despite the teacher's thin appearance, he was incredibly heavy and Jake had made slow progress. But if he had delayed another few seconds, then Mr. Falconer would now be lying under half a ton of rubble. A support beam had burned through, causing the roof to crash in, and with it the contents of the classroom above.

The school principal, Mr. Harris, watched with Jake as the ambulance carrying Falconer pulled away, its lights flashing and siren whooping. Falconer had momentarily regained consciousness and mumbled

A Meeting in the Dark

incoherently about Jake glowing green. The paramedics assumed it was a side effect of the traumatic ordeal.

"You're a brave boy," said Mr. Harris. The firemen could find no immediate cause of the fire, and the principal was well aware of Jake's reputation as a troublemaker. But because he'd pulled the teacher out of the flames, without a doubt saving his life, he couldn't exactly accuse him of arson. But it felt strange calling the bully a hero.

Jake mulled things over as he walked home. The green haze coming from him had definitely been real, and not a hallucination brought on by the asphyxiating smoke, that much he was sure about. The glow had increased with his anger but then slowly ebbed away when he calmed down.

But what was it? And why couldn't he feel the heat himself? When he pulled Mr. Falconer from the conflagration the shimmering green energy field had reappeared, covering him completely. Fire had rolled across the wall next to him, and he hadn't felt the flames lick across his face.

Jake would be the first to admit he wasn't a straight-A student, but he certainly wasn't stupid. He knew that he shouldn't have been able to stand in a room where the metal chairs were melting into puddles. No matter how much he twisted the facts, they all pointed back to the previous night when he visited that Web site and clicked on the radioactive button. He'd seen the monitor warp—that couldn't have been an optical illusion as he'd originally assumed. Somehow, he had been given the power to produce radiation, and apparently to control it with his anger and fear. Jake decided that when he got home, he was going to get to the bottom of the mystery one way or another.

News travels fast. Almost at light speed if it moves from your school to your parents. Jake hadn't even inserted his key in the lock before his mother swung the door open and grabbed him in an emotional hug.

"Jacob! You're okay!"

"Yes, I'm fine," he managed as he pushed her away.

"Brave thing you did," his father said, standing a little farther back. "Just glad you're okay! It gave my heart a start when I heard the news. Running into a burning building took some guts!"

Jake shrugged in response. "Yeah, whatever. I have to go and get changed. I reek of smoke." He extracted himself from his parents' hugs and questions and headed upstairs. After a long shower he quietly entered his bedroom, twisted the lock on the door, and booted up his computer.

"Let's find out what the heck's going on," he mumbled.

His fingers were a blur across the keyboard as he logged onto his e-mail. Seconds later the mail program appeared with the mysterious e-mail from his namesake.

A Meeting in the Dark

He had moved to click on the message when it was suddenly pushed down the list by the arrival of a new one. Bold letters read:

"CONGRATULATIONS ON YOUR NEW SUPER-POWERS!"

Jake felt his heart beat faster. "What is this?"

He felt his hand tremble as he clicked on the e-mail. A larger window opened up, and he quickly read through it. "Now that you have experienced the awesome powers available to you, take your next step on the path to world domination by meeting here, thirty minutes from now."

A small JPEG graphic at the bottom of the e-mail depicted a map. It took Jake a few seconds to realize that it showed the way from his house to the abandoned steel mill. Jake looked back up to the screen and noticed the time had already started counting down the passing seconds.

Jake wasn't naive enough to agree to meet in person a stranger he'd met over the Internet, but he couldn't ignore what had happened in the classroom. The more he thought about it, the more it made sense. Somehow, he had inherited some kind of radioactive power from the Villain.net Web site. He tried to recall what he knew about radioactive material. The side effects were not pleasant; he'd seen enough monster movies to know that. He worried that he might get sick from radioactive poisoning.

The timer now read twenty-eight minutes. He figured it would take at least twenty minutes on his bike to get to the steel mill, and walking out the front door would raise questions from his family and waste time.

Jake thumped a fist decisively against his desk. He had to know what was happening to him. He moved to the window and slid it open. The back porch was just underneath his room and offered a perfect step to climb out on. From there he lowered himself to the ground, dropping the last few feet with practiced ease. Making sure nobody was looking from the living room windows, Jake ran across to the toolshed.

His fingers shook as he unscrambled the combination lock on the shed door and pulled out his mountain bike. A shovel fell against the wall with a loud clatter as the bike dislodged it. Jake reached forward to secure the tool before it made any more noise. A quick glance toward the house confirmed nobody had heard. He started to close the door, then hesitated; walking into the steel-works at night, alone, was ill advised. He had no idea who, or what, would be waiting for him. Just on the edge of the shed's workbench was a heavy iron wrench. Jake picked it up and weighed the tool in his hand.

"You'll work," he mumbled and he tucked the wrench in his belt.

* * *

A Meeting in the Dark

The factory was dark and forbidding. Jake had been here many times before, but never alone. Now the dark ruins looked oppressive and unwelcoming. He drew a long breath and tried to imagine that there was only one threat in the darkness: *him*. Everybody else had better watch out. Feeling a little more confident, Jake dismounted and followed the security fence. He knew where the rips in the rusty mesh were.

Beyond the fence, crumbling brick walls several stories high flanked the narrow roadways around the mill. Corrugated metal sheets clanked in the gentle breeze. The whirl of his bike's spokes echoed through the complex. His hand touched the wrench lodged in his belt, and he silently berated himself for not bringing a flashlight. Ivy had covered most of the buildings, while the weather had stripped away roofs, making the first stars of the night visible beyond.

Jake froze as his foot clattered aside a rusted oilcan. It bounced in the darkness, sounding unnaturally loud. He felt a chill run up his spine and could have sworn the air temperature had suddenly dropped.

"Congratulations, Hunter," purred a voice from the darkness behind him.

Jake wheeled around, dropping his bike and sliding out the wrench in one fluid movement. He heard slow, mocking clapping from the shadows. It sounded like bricks being banged together.

"Very good. Reflexes like a cat," continued the voice.

"Who are you?" Jake demanded.

"I'm your new best friend."

The darkness shifted as a figure stepped from the deepest shadows. He was much taller than Jake. Faint moonlight reflected off steel struts that braced both legs and disappeared in a pair of black boots with countless buckles on them. His arms were bare and looked to have the texture of stone. The rest of the stranger was clad in matte black, but even in the dim light Jake could see the man's chest was well defined with muscles. A short black cape hung over his shoulders, and when the moonlight caught it, it seemed to glitter like a snakeskin. A wide hood covered his head, obscuring any features. He stood and appraised Jake with a slight tilt of the head. When he crossed his arms, they made the sound of stone grating against stone as they moved.

Jake held his ground, although he wanted to jump on his bike and scurry away.

"You can call me Basilisk!" The figure's voice reverberated dramatically among the deserted buildings.

After years of picking on kids with stupid names, Jake couldn't help but smile. "*Basilisk?* What kind of name is that?"

"One you will respect!"

Basilisk took a step forward, his boots thumping heavily

on the ground as he drew himself to his full height. Jake gasped; he hadn't been aware the figure was slouching until now. Basilisk must have been almost seven feet tall, and egg-shaped eyes flared neon blue under his hood.

Despite himself, Jake let out a whimper of fear and took a step backward as he lifted the wrench, ready to strike. Basilisk boomed with humorless laughter.

"Oh, very good. Feisty and aggressive. Those traits will serve you well."

"Take one more step and I'll slug you across the head!" Jake warned.

A beam of concentrated light shot from Basilisk's finger, as fine as string, but the moment it struck the wrench the tool glowed bright red and smoldered in Jake's hand. He let go of it with a yelp.

"How'd you do that?" he said while sucking his burned fingers. "Did you get those powers off a Web site by any chance?"

"No. I was born with them. But I did send you that e-mail. You were given a gift. A temporary gift to be used how you see fit. And I have been watching you."

"Why?"

"I saw how you used your powers for rage and revenge. Burning down your classroom was very wicked," Basilisk's voice became thoughtful. "Although you lost points for pulling out that pain-in-the-neck teacher of yours. But you were close to perfect, allowing your actions to be guided by your feelings. Controlled anger is the mightiest weapon."

Jake's questions tumbled out at once. "I want to know exactly what you've done to me. Are there any side effects, like radiation poisoning? Is it going to happen to me again?"

Basilisk regarded him silently for a moment. "How did it feel? Knowing you controlled such a destructive force?"

Jake was thrown by the question. He had to admit that he'd felt a thrill tremble through him when he realized that he had been the source of the fire. It had made him feel terrified too, but there was no way he was going to admit weakness to this stranger.

"It was cool." Jake reflected that that was an inappropriate choice of words.

"It's in your blood. Wielding power is part of who you are; of what you've become. You have the ability to rule. An ability few men possess."

"Is that right?" said Jake skeptically, though it was a great sales pitch to his ego.

"The Web site, Villain.net, is a portal to channel your anger and fear. If you use it right, we can be truly unstoppable. You can have not just a single power. Imagine hundreds at your disposal."

Jake's mind was now running quickly through his options, a form of mental gymnastics he wasn't used to.

A Meeting in the Dark

Basilisk didn't look like the mild-mannered do-gooders that Jake had seen in the movies. He looked every bit the sinister bad guy, and that sent a conflict of emotions through Jake's mind. Of course, running with the good guys would be just plain dull, but this guy seemed like major trouble—and trouble was something Jake was good at detecting.

"So through the Web site I can just click and use any of those powers when I want to?"

"You can download them, yes. Anytime you want. But, of course, you don't get something for nothing."

Jake shook his head; he knew it was too good to be true. "You want money?"

Basilisk unfolded his arms and held out his hands in a "stop" gesture. "Not from you. I want your services. If you wish to possess these powers, then you must help me. Let me be your mentor, your trainer."

"Why me?"

"Because you are unique. You have undreamed potential."

"And what would I have to do?"

"Assist me, and see the world like you've never seen it before. It would be like a unique adventure camp." Basilisk held out his hand as if to shake Jake's. "Do we have a deal?"

Jake hesitated; this all seemed wrong. At school Jake was goaded into actions that he knew weren't right, like letting Scuffer persuade him to use the virus. Jake felt it was a sign of being weak willed, even if his friends seemed to respect him more for doing it.

His eyes scanned the dark factory around him. If he wanted to, he could run. But an element of curiosity held him in place, even now. Basilisk was offering a fresh start—unlimited power and an opportunity to leave his boring life behind. Basilisk seemed like the bad-tempered kind, but that was something Jake was used to dealing with. He felt scared, and he knew fear led to weakness. The kids he picked on were frightened of him and that made them weak, prime targets for bullying. He took a deep breath—although he was scared, he was no coward.

He reached out and shook Basilisk's hand. It dwarfed his own. His skin felt like granite, and as it closed around Jake's, he could feel that it was stone. His astonishment with the rocky skin lasted for a second before the powerful grip stopped short of crushing every bone in his hand. Jake didn't make a murmur, and shook life back into his hand when Basilisk turned and strode into the darkness.

"We leave now," said Basilisk.

"Leave? Where? My parents don't even—"

Basilisk spun around on his heels, his eyes flaring deep blue. "Your parents? I am offering you a chance to help me rule the world, and you're worrying about getting home late? If I am to make you a king, then you will learn from me—not them!"

A Meeting in the Dark

Basilisk turned away and continued into the darkness. Jake realized that this guy was crazy and he could be dangerous. If Jake had not sampled the superpower firsthand, then he would have turned away. But he had, and now he needed to quench his thirst for that power again. He followed.

"You never told me where we're going, Bas."

"Traveling!" said Basilisk. And on cue a small vehicle was illuminated at the end of the factory floor. At first Jake mistook it for a sleek sports car, as it had the graceful curves of a Porsche. But as he got closer it was clear the vehicle was larger and had no wheels. Instead it sat on three landing skis. A series of narrow fins ran along the back of the craft, giving it the appearance of a menacing shark. As Basilisk approached, a pair of gull-wing doors hissed open, revealing two plush seats inside. Basilisk hauled himself into the driver's seat, and gestured for Jake to sit alongside.

"Wow!" Jake said, running his hands along the black carbon-fiber bodywork. "What is this?"

"It's my own invention, a SkyKar. And if you don't mind, we have an appointment to keep. Get in."

Basilisk seemed to sense Jake's hesitation. "Hunter, this is a mission I need your help with. This is where your training begins. After this you will be returning home until I need you again."

Jake took a deep breath and nodded. He slid into the

seat. The doors automatically folded down, and the dashboard lit up in an array of digital displays around a central monitor screen. A Head-Up Display (HUD) projected against the windshield gave all manner of flight data.

"You will need to buckle your harness," Basilisk said as a rising engine hum vibrated through the SkyKar. Jake looked down at his seat, his fingers scrambling for the seat belt. He found one strap, but before he could locate the other the vehicle tilted upward and accelerated at a phenomenal speed. Jake was pushed back in his seat by the sudden g-force and felt the breath crushed out of him.

"And never call me *Bas* again."

The SkyKar leveled out and the intense effect of the g-force vanished from Jake's body as quickly as a blanket being pulled away. He gasped for breath, both hands gripping the dashboard for support.

"I warned you to strap yourself in," commented Basilisk.

"A little more warning next time would be preferred," snarled Jake. He peered out of the curved windows. "We're flying!" It was a much better view than through the small portholes of airplanes; he could see the towns below, laid out in yellow and white pinpricks like a mirror to the stars above.

A Meeting in the Dark

"Flying? You haven't experienced anything yet," Basilisk said as he pivoted a monitor screen to face Jake. On it was the banner Villain.net, and a range of icons beneath that; many more than last time. "As a minion you get to choose four powers. It's a touch screen."

Jake eagerly examined the display. As before, every icon depicted a stick figure in a pose, some with lines coming from their hands, others with lines from their head. There was the occasional symbol that Jake recognized from playing on his Xbox: the radioactive sign and another he was pretty sure meant biohazard. He shuddered at the thought of that one: would he come out with oozing lumps of pus like a giant zit?

"What do they all do?"

For the first time, Basilisk hesitated. "Ah, yes. That's a slight, uh, *design* problem with the site." He faced Jake, but even this close his features remained hidden in the shadows of his hood. "A lot of the elements of this site were stolen and we don't have descriptions of all the icons. We only know a few. You'll just have to make an educated guess."

"Stolen? From where?"

"Downloading superpowers through the Internet is not the same as downloading your favorite song, you know. Just choose instead of asking questions."

Jake looked back at the screen. With no key to what

the symbols could be, he indiscriminately stabbed his finger at four of the icons. As before, the surface of the monitor writhed like a living thing and formed a thin tendril toward his head. It was an unsettling experience, over in a second.

"What did you select?" Basilisk asked keenly.

"Um . . . I don't really know. I just randomly hit things."

"What? You should *think* about your actions. Being thoughtless will get you killed!"

Jake glared at the hooded figure and felt, not for the first time, an intense dislike for the enigmatic Basilisk. Then he began to experience a crawling sensation in his hands, racing toward his fingertips. Basilisk suddenly stretched across the dashboard and hit a button. Instantly the sensation in Jake's fingers vanished.

"What just happened?"

"I activated the power dampener. Otherwise you might have blown my SkyKar out of the air. And since you don't know if you have flying powers or not, I didn't think it was worth the risk. Besides, the vehicle's not insured."

"Power dampener?"

"It inhibits superpowers." Basilisk reached in the side of his seat and pulled out a pair of handcuffs with a digital keypad in the center to lock them. "Normally you need a generator the size of a house to dampen even the most basic powers. But my latest creation crams it all into a small chip. I used the same technology in these.

A Meeting in the Dark

Cuff a superhero and—*zap!*—their powers have been nullified. Just sold the first batch to a criminal called Tempest. Good luck to him."

Jake shook his head. This all seemed crazy. On top of everything else it looked as if Basilisk was a nutty inventor who sold his creations to other supervillains.

"We'll be at our destination in a couple of hours," Basilisk continued, "so sit back and enjoy the ride. When we arrive you'll have ample time to vent your anger!"

"But I'm not angry."

"You will be," said Basilisk with a trace of mirth.

Jake decided not to ask any further questions, as he figured they wouldn't be answered anyway. He sat back and enjoyed the view. It was probably also best not to mention he didn't have his passport.

The SkyKar shimmied, and Jake felt his stomach lurch. He must have drifted asleep. He opened his eyes and was greeted by the rays of dawn peeking over the horizon. He could feel that they were descending. A quick glance at his watch told him that more than two hours had passed.

Basilisk hit a button on the control panel, and the words "AUTO PILOT" illuminated. The gull-wing doors flipped open in tandem, and Basilisk half stood on his seat.

"Are you ready?"

Jake rubbed the sleep from his eyes. "Ready for what?"

Basilisk snapped his hand out and unfastened Jake's seat belt.

"Ready to *fly*!"

Jake opened his mouth to respond—but before he could, Basilisk's heavy boot slammed into his chest. Jake scrambled to hold on to *anything* as he was kicked from his seat and fell from the SkyKar.

It was an odd experience. The descending SkyKar appeared to move away from Jake in slow motion as he fell at a slightly faster speed. The roar of wind bellowed past his ears and tore at his clothes. He managed to spin around onto his chest, and saw, below him, dawn light glinting off the glass towers of a sprawling building complex etched out in a rocky desert.

It didn't look as if it would cushion Jake's fall.

Basilisk suddenly glided into view, in full control of his dive. He zipped past Jake as agile as a hummingbird.

"Jake, you can fly!"

"How do you know? You don't know what powers I got," Jake screamed back through the wind. "I could have downloaded a superpower that helps me fall!"

"I lied. I know what *some* of the icons mean. I configured the system to make sure flying was one of your chosen powers. It's something I've learned at a high cost. I've seen too many sidekicks splattered!"

A Meeting in the Dark

The structure below was looming larger than ever, now fully taking up Jake's peripheral vision. He closed his eyes, and thrust his hands down as if to cushion his fall. He could almost imagine the roaring wind in his ears had stopped.

In fact the wind *had* stopped.

Jake opened his eyes. He was no longer rushing to meet the ground, but instead hovered over the complex. Basilisk hung alongside, so in control that the wind hadn't even displaced his hood. The SkyKar suddenly thundered between them as it continued a preprogrammed descent, and Jake wavered slightly as he was caught in the vehicle's wake of displaced air.

"I can fly!" he said in awe.

"You can do so much more than that, Hunter."

Jake glanced at Basilisk. He was not used to positive comments from *anybody*.

"Your powers feed off your fear and anger. That is why they manifested when you were angry with your teacher. Reach inside and embrace those feelings. Use them to your advantage!"

Those feelings were familiar. He'd heard the old adage that bullies are just cowards—and he knew that to be true. Every time he picked on a kid he felt a knot of fear that he might get punched back. That's what made it all exciting.

Jake's arms and legs flicked out as he caught his

balance. Now the rush of possibilities flowed through him as he sensed the power at his fingertips. He remembered what his dad had once told him, after he'd been in trouble for the hundredth time.

"Your future's what you make of it."

Jake realized that the fruitcake in the cape, flying alongside him, was giving him the opportunity to create a fabulous future. Jake was determined not to mess up this opportunity as he had so many others.

"Okay, what are we doing here? Where are we?"

"The subcontinent of India." Basilisk jabbed a finger down. "That is a top secret, high-security, scientific development lab. Inside, they have developed something called the Core Probe, a robotic mole capable of burrowing straight to the earth's core. And we want it."

"We do? Why?"

"For power and glory!" Basilisk saw that Jake didn't seem motivated. He shook his head. "Because it's essential to my plan! In a few seconds the SkyKar is going to trip the security defenses, and then things will get very interesting."

"Interesting how?"

Basilisk shook his head, just as a warbling alarm sounded from below, echoing across the complex. Jake could see people and armed vehicles deployed from a hangar just to one side of the complex.

"They have guns!"

A Meeting in the Dark

Basilisk pointed. "They have *missiles*."

Jake hadn't spotted a pair of flatbed trucks camouflaged in a thicket of ornamental trees. Gimbal-mounted missile launchers on the trucks spun to face them, and twin flashes made the vehicles lurch as a pair of rockets shot out.

Jake felt a flood of adrenaline course through him, heightening his senses. "What do we do?"

Basilisk's voice was as smooth as honey, belying the fun he was having. "Now we fight!"

With that, Basilisk powered toward the ground, but Jake couldn't avert his eyes from the missiles that were almost on top of him.

"This is it," Jake thought, "I'm going to die."

The First Steps

It was difficult for Jake to explain how he knew what to do; his every action had just seemed natural. The missiles had been so close that Jake could make out the symbols on the red nose cones warning that they were high-explosive devices. Jake held his hands out, palms up, and the air glistened around his body—both projectiles exploded in front of him in a fierce blast of orange and midnight black that set the sky afire.

Flames curled around him, but it was as if he were trapped in a giant bubble. The air shimmered as the fire probed for a weakness. Jake was hurled head over heels before he caught his balance. Seconds later the fireball had burned itself out, and tiny fragments of shrapnel rained down.

"Wow!"

A distinctive pinging noise came from below. Jake glanced down to see four army jeeps had swiveled their machine guns toward him and opened fire. The high-caliber bullets bounced off his invisible shield. It occurred to him that he didn't know how long this shield would hold, so he'd better act fast. Already the two mobile missile platforms had teams of men reloading them.

Jake pivoted his body down as though he was diving and stretched forward. In the blink of an eye he was zeroing down toward the nearest jeep. The soldiers manning the machine guns made an admirable attempt at tracking his progress as Jake swooped low, pulling himself horizontally mere inches off the ground and powering toward them like a bullet, kicking up a cloud of dust in his wake.

Gunfire tore the ground around him but ricocheted harmlessly off Jake's shield. In three seconds flat he ploughed into the jeep. Some of the soldiers leaped clear as Jake rammed the vehicle sidelong.

He pulled himself to a halt above the ground to watch as the car rapidly bounced sideways, unidentifiable parts flying off with each impact with the ground. The jeep covered fifty feet before slamming into another gun jeep—whose desperate soldiers trained their machine-gun fire on the metal hulk in a futile attempt to stop the collision.

Jake whooped with delight as the spinning jeep toppled the second vehicle over onto its side, spilling the men everywhere. From the impact with the other vehicle, Jake's "bowled" jeep leaped in the air, spiraling out of control—before it smashed through a second-floor mirrored window on the main building behind.

"Wow!" he yelled. It was like living in a computer game. The excitement was tangible, and it made him feel more alive than he ever had.

The troops that had been thrown off the jeeps had the presence of mind to flee. Jake felt flushed with anger—how dare they shoot at him?

He recalled Basilisk's instructions and channeled his indignation. He extended his hand and felt a pulse of heat travel down his arm, and a split second later a green snake of radioactive energy shot from his hand, twisting through the air like Silly String until it struck the fleeing men. They fell down on the spot, instantly breaking Jake's concentration. He was filled with dread. He hadn't meant to kill them. But faint groaning from the prone figures assured him they were still alive.

More gunfire churned the ground around him, and bullets pinged off his shield. He twisted around to see the remaining two jeeps jouncing across the desert rocks toward him. Beyond, he could see that the crews of two missile platforms had finished reloading, and it was only a matter of time before they fired again. He looked around for Basilisk, but the villain was nowhere to be seen.

Jake was alone and right in the center of it all.

A sudden tug of conscience asked him how he'd wound up in this lethal situation. He nudged the thoughts away; he didn't have time to daydream. He took to the air and raced toward the missile trucks. He looked and felt as if he'd been flying all his life. However, Jake was focused on only one thing: destroying the trucks before they fired their next batch of missiles at him. Years of playing games on his consoles had drummed basic strategy into his brain.

He passed between the jeeps like a rocket. One gun team had the presence of mind to stop firing—but the other continued, bullets tearing across the jeep opposite and shredding the armored vehicle. The tires were blown out as the vehicle's occupants dived for cover from the friendly fire.

The missile operating crews didn't have time to respond as the boy tore toward them. A haze of green radioactive energy blossomed from his outstretched fingers and blasted one of the flatbeds. It folded in two in the middle, the missile rig collapsing onto the ground with a groan of twisted metal.

The commander of the second truck punched the fire control in panic before he sprinted away. The missile arced wildly in the sky as Jake hurled another energy blast. This time the rear section of the flatbed was consumed, and the entire vehicle angled down and sideways with such a force it flipped the flatbed truck onto its side.

Jake pulled up from his flight, and found he had to run several feet across the dirt to stop himself from falling over, just like the speed change experienced when running off an escalator. He surveyed his handiwork with wide eyes, as rapidly cooling metal plinked.

"That was cool! Now where's that hooded idiot?" He turned to the building, half expecting Basilisk to step out of concealment after Jake had won the fight.

Instead he faced the devil-red tip of a heat-seeking missile. The faint trail of exhaust smoke indicated it had just completed a revolution in the sky. Jake threw his arms up in panic. . . .

BLAM! The missile exploded right in front of him, fire and shrapnel bouncing inches from his face as his force field kicked in. This time the energy from the detonation pushed him backward. Jake felt as though a gigantic fist had punched him. He was lifted clean off his feet and hurled against trees in the glade that had camouflaged the missile launchers.

He knew he'd let his guard down—a stupid mistake he had seen in others during countless schoolyard fights. The moment somebody's guard dropped, usually when they thought they were winning, was the perfect time to strike. And that lapse in judgment had almost cost him his life.

It felt painful to move, but Jake pulled himself upright only to see the final armored jeep bouncing toward him.

"I'd forgotten about that," he mumbled, hoping he had

the strength to do something about it. But the explosion had made his head feel woozy, like being woken from a deep sleep.

"Don't move!" the Enforcers yelled, training their M16 rifles on him. A third soldier rotated the massive 16mm gun to face Jake, his finger lightly resting on the dual triggers. "Stand up! Slowly."

"Don't move or stand up? Make up your mind," Jake said groggily.

The soldiers were at a loss. Five of their heavy perimeter defenses had been destroyed by a flying figure that had hurled energy bolts. And that figure turned out to be a young boy in an Ironfist T-shirt.

"I said, on your feet, boy," confirmed the soldier Jake assumed was in charge. "Hands on your head. Don't try any funny business."

Jake's vision was returning along with his strength, and with it, a familiar feeling of resentment. Why should he allow himself to be bullied by these guys, even if they were wielding guns? Jake slowly climbed to his feet, crossing his arms over his head.

"What now?" he asked with a defiant sneer.

The soldiers swapped nervous glances as burning chunks of leaves drifted from the trees above.

"Those weapons look a little hot for you," Jake said casually, remembering Basilisk's trick with the wrench. The tree trunks behind suddenly erupted into

flames, startling the troopers. They raised their weapons menacingly.

"I told you not to move!"

"I haven't lifted a finger."

"And not to spe—" The guard's words turned into a shriek of pain as his gun glowed red. Both soldiers dropped their weapons. The guy on the truck released the 16mm triggers as they burned his fingers. The steel chassis of the jeep started to smolder and the paint bubble. Seconds later the padded seats erupted into flames.

"You better run," whispered Jake as the ground under his feet grew black and leaked acrid smoke.

The three men regarded Jake with horror. With the blazing trees behind, they thought a demon had risen— and they certainly weren't getting paid enough to fight the supernatural. They fled as fast as they could, never looking back.

This brought a smile to Jake's face; it was much more fun than anything he'd done before. When he had been younger, he'd played with toys, crashing his cars first into one another, and then smashing them with his dad's hammer to make the destruction more authentic. But now that he could do this for real, whole cities could be his playground. Basilisk was definitely onto something when he spoke of power. Jake liked this feeling and wanted more.

With that in mind, he rose a few inches into the air

and flew across to the complex, where the alarms were still squawking loudly, and an automated voice warned of "intruders" in multiple languages. Jake felt confident as he entered the building in search of his mentor.

The large glass entrance hall must have looked stunning five minutes earlier, splendidly decorated with plasma screens, glass sculptures, and fine water features. But now smashed monitors sparked lifelessly, and the fountains were splintered beyond repair, water flooding across the floor.

A proud sign declaring: THE INDIAN INSTITUTE OF ADVANCED TECHNOLOGY had been shot up. Bullet holes riddled the walls and ceiling. Rifles lay discarded on the floor but there was no sign of any bodies, only a fine layer of dust and chunks of gray rubble.

The incessant alarm drew him back to the situation. The noise started to aggravate him, but he couldn't see where it was coming from. Instead he cocked his head, hoping to hear Basilisk's path of destruction. Sure enough, a distant scream followed by a loud crash got Jake's attention, and he ran in that direction.

The corridors were wide and straight, with the occasional signs of a skirmish, but again no evidence of the hapless guards caught in Basilisk's path. Jake turned a corner—and a vending machine next to him exploded in a shower of flames. Punctured soda cans clattered everywhere; streams of fizzy drink propelled them across the floor. Jake felt a firm hand pull him sideways into a doorway.

"Keep your head down," Basilisk commanded as another powerful laser bolt struck the frame above them, cracking wood and clattering plaster dust into Jake's hair.

"What is it?"

"They've activated one of the Institute's military research projects and turned it on us. Something my petrifying powers have no effect upon. Some kind of RoboSoldier."

Jake risked a peek around the corner. An eight-foot-tall Goliath blocked the end of the corridor, with several white-coated scientists cowering behind it. The RoboSoldier was essentially a humanoid shape, with smooth flowing metal skin that bent with its limbs to conceal any moving parts. The head was a simple dome with an inverted "V" slit visor where the eyes should be. Somebody had drawn a pair of cartoon eyes above the machine's visor, but it didn't make it any less intimidating.

Jake saw a pulse of energy, like a camera flash, in the RoboSoldier's eyes, and then a chunky yellow laser fired out and ripped away another piece of masonry close to his ear.

Jake felt debris bounce from his face. "It's going to

blast through the wall to get us if we just hide here! Do something!"

"I can't. My energy blasts aren't strong enough, and my petrifying powers work only on living targets."

"Living? You mean you can't do anything about that giant robot at the end of the corridor?"

Basilisk's voice changed to a caustic tone. "Yes, I can *hide* while my accomplice selects which of his panoply of powers to use."

Jake bit back a sarcastic reply, annoyed by Basilisk's fancy words. Already he was getting tired of the villain's sneering tone. Without willing it, Jake felt his hands burn as the radioactive power took over. He rolled into the corridor, like he'd seen the heroes do in movies, and unleashed a tangle of radioactive streamers at the mechanoid.

It was a perfect hit. A bulletin board next to the RoboSoldier burst into flame, as did several ceiling tiles. Then the radioactive luminance died away, and Jake gasped.

"Oh no!"

The machine was unharmed—and Jake was left crouching in the corridor, a sitting duck. He leaped back into concealment as another laser bolt bored into the ceramic tiled floor, carving a trench where he had been.

"It didn't work!"

"Of course not! I told you energy blasts wouldn't be enough. That thing is built to fight through a nuclear war. What else have you got?"

"Just a shield, and I can fly."

A footstep rang out from the end of the corridor. This time Basilisk risked a glance over Jake's shoulder. The machine was taking long measured steps down the hall toward them, each footfall so heavy the tiles cracked underfoot.

"Think!" bellowed Basilisk with an edge of panic in his voice. "You downloaded four powers. What is the fourth?"

Jake drew a blank, and shook his head. What could it be? The flying, the force field, and the radioactive blasts had materialized without any conscious effort from Jake, so why hadn't the fourth?

Another set of thunderous steps brought the machine closer, and another blast clipped the edge of the doorway.

"Time is running out, Hunter. I hadn't factored this into my plan. Think quickly."

The clipped sentences reminded Jake of his math teacher, Mr. Rutledge, who always took great delight in embarrassing him in front of the class by asking him the answers to impossible problems. The world already had enough Mr. Rutledges, and Jake hoped he'd have these powers one day in class so he could use them against the creep.

The First Steps

Jake was so consumed by his vision of extracting revenge on his math teacher that he didn't realize he had caused his fourth power to manifest.

"Jake! Look at your hands!" said Basilisk.

Jake held them up. They appeared to be wet, with a liquid dripping from every pore. A drop landed on Basilisk's arm with a hiss as it burned into his stone skin.

"Acid," Jake said in surprise.

He quickly moved his hands so as not to burn Basilisk any further, and extended them away from his own body. Jake took a deep breath and jumped back into the corridor.

RoboSoldier was halfway down the passageway, its head twisted toward Jake. Jake stretched his fingers as he held his hands aloft, and twin globs of acid spat from his palms. One globule hit the mechanoid's chest and instantly began chewing the armor away in a cloud of hissing smoke. Jake's second shot struck across the robot's visor—just as he saw it flare with energy.

The acid melted the eye slit on contact—at the precise moment RoboSoldier primed and fired its laser. With no visor opening, the laser blew apart the machine's head from the inside. The headless body staggered a few steps, but with its guidance processors fried it could do nothing else but topple over like a drunk, smashing a dozen floor tiles.

Jake took in his victory openmouthed, then looked at

his hands, which had returned to normal. "Awesome," he murmured under his breath.

Basilisk strode past him, confident once again. The knot of scientists at the end of the corridor cowered and raised their hands in surrender as their eyes darted from Basilisk to their defeated guardian.

"Now tell me," rumbled Basilisk, his eyes flaring a malevolent blue, "where is the Core Probe?"

A bespectacled scientist pushed his way defiantly forward. "You'll never have it! It is in the vault, and nobody will supply you with *that* code!"

Basilisk grabbed the man by the neck, and lifted him off his feet. The scientist gurgled and thumped Basilisk's arm. The villain ensured everybody was watching, and then his eyes flared brightly from within the recesses of the hood.

With a cracking noise the scientist's skin took on the same dull sheen as Basilisk's own hands, and his thrashing limbs became rigid. The man was being petrified—turned to stone in front of everyone. Jake jumped at a noise like a balloon bursting, as the scientist suddenly turned to fine dust in Basilisk's hand. The charcoal powder and tiny stone fragments washed over the startled witnesses.

Jake thought about what he'd just seen. That explained the gray ash throughout the complex; the guards had never stood a chance. He felt a chill run through him. This was a level of violence that he'd never encountered before. When he actually calmed down enough to realize what he was doing, he felt a panic attack coming on, and his thoughts briefly turned to Scuffer and his destructive nature.

"So, who wants to open the vault for me?" Basilisk asked pleasantly, as if he were ordering food in a restaurant.

The terrified scientists all offered. Anything to get out of this predicament alive.

Basilisk had ordered Jake to be rear guard as he selected one of the scientists, a petite Indian woman, to lead the way. Jake frowned but complied; he really didn't like the way Basilisk told him what to do.

Told, not *asked*.

They entered a huge circular development chamber that was equipped with computers, scopes, and screens for projects unfathomable to Jake. He remained silent and watched over the scientists, who were clearly too scared to show any bravado.

The woman keyed in a code on a small keypad adjacent to a huge circular vault door. Pneumatic rams slammed into place, drawing open the ten-foot-thick bombproof door like a cork being pulled from a wine bottle. Inside the vault stood the Core Probe, supported on a wheeled frame so it could be moved around the lab.

At first glance, the device resembled a ten-foot-tall thimble, with the curved underside pointing down. But on closer inspection the curve was a giant glasslike bowl with an array of lasers behind it, all pointing at the convex surface. The exterior surface of the probe was covered in heat-resistant matte-black tiles, with a dozen caterpillar tracks running the length of the machine to give it traction beneath the earth.

Basilisk ordered the scientists to wheel the probe out of the vault and toward a set of loading doors on the far side of the lab. The petite woman rested her hand on another keypad mounted on the loading doors, but hesitated as though debating whether she should open it. All Basilisk had to do was stand behind her; his shadow was enough to prompt her into entering the code.

Outside, Basilisk's SkyKar was hovering over a circular helicopter landing pad. On Basilisk's orders the scientists attached the Core Probe to a harness dangling from the vehicle's underbelly.

"A job well done, Hunter," said Basilisk. "Do you want to deal with the witnesses, or should I?"

Jake wondered how many people Basilisk had killed to get this device. Was it worth all the carnage? Jake would gladly step into a fair fight and cause untold damage—but he drew the line at killing. Was that what it took to be successful? He looked at the frightened group and nodded.

The First Steps

"I'll sort it out."

Basilisk grunted his approval and soared up to the cockpit of the SkyKar. Jake swallowed hard and turned to face the prisoners, and he hoped his nervousness didn't show.

"All of you, get in the lab. NOW," he bellowed in his most threatening voice. The scientists shuffled back through the loading-bay doors. He followed the group into the lab and closed the doors behind him, giving a quick nod to Basilisk, who was watching intently from the SkyKar.

Jake turned to the pale faces. The warm seep of the radiation pulsed through him, powered by his fear rather than anger.

The scientists' lives were in his hands.

1011101000010010101011001001101

Grand Designs

The return journey was a little slower due to the additional weight of the Core Probe slung beneath the SkyKar.

Jake was too wrapped up in his thoughts to acknowledge Basilisk's occasional compliment about Jake's villainy. He tried to shake the thoughts from his mind that people had just died. The fighting was a lot of fun, but completely beyond the realms of normality, which had made it seem like a game. Yet people had lost their lives. The more Jake thought about the last twenty-four hours, the more confused he felt. He wanted some answers. Halfway through the flight he couldn't bottle up the questions any longer.

"Who are you? In the real world, I mean. Or what are you? And why did you give me these powers?" A hundred other thoughts rattled through his mind, but he knew there was no time for them now.

Basilisk gave a low chuckle. "Only now do you ask? Incredible. You have flown, battled a robotic soldier, and fired radiation blasts from your hands, and not once did you question your abilities."

Grand Designs

Jake thought about that. Of course the "how and why" had been floating through his mind, but the sheer thrill of his adventure had pushed them aside.

"As I said before, Hunter: this is all in your blood. I've been watching you for some time, and what you have done is something you find very natural, I wager."

Jake felt uncomfortable that Basilisk may have been spying on him. Had he been following Jake to see if he had what it took to be a criminal? Was this some kind of test? But he had to admit that wielding the powers took little effort, as though he had been able to do it his whole life.

Basilisk continued, talking over Jake's thoughts. "As to who I am, isn't it obvious?"

"Sure, you're a guy who likes dressing up and has a Web site that gives me superpowers. Even I know that's not normal."

"The costume or the powers? I am what the authorities like to call a supervillain."

Jake was expecting that answer, but it still felt odd to hear it and he tried to suppress a grin. "Like in the movies? Threatening to conquer the world?"

"Exactly. Where do you think they get those ideas? It's been happening throughout history. Real life is the best form of inspiration. A film producer once modeled his main villain after me."

Jake frowned. "What was the film?"

"Let's just say there was no sequel," Basilisk replied ominously. "There used to be many of us, each with separate plans for domination, blackmail, destruction, and revenge. Each of us who remains still wants power in some shape or form."

"That must get complicated. Don't you ever end up crossing paths or having the same ideas?"

Basilisk grunted. Jake had a feeling he'd touched a nerve. It was several seconds before Basilisk continued. "Our numbers are thinning, and we saw that by banding together we could recruit others to our way of life. We tried a variety of recruitment methods, but they failed to work. We moved to cyberspace and tried to recruit that way, but our techniques were primitive and had to be scrapped. Then Villain.net was born from those digital ashes. The perfect lure for young, impressionable minds, don't you think?"

"How many more of you bad guys are there still around?"

"I think you mean 'us' bad guys. But 'bad' is such a clichéd black-and-white view of the world. We just have different opinions. And when those opinions conflict with the majority's cherished beliefs, then they label us as 'the bad guys.'"

"But what about good and evil?"

"It is not a battle between good and evil, there is no such thing. It is merely a battle of wills, a battle for power. Those who are brave and smart enough will win it. When countries go to war how can one be good and one be evil? The populations of those countries both think that they're on the side of justice. Would you consider yourself evil?"

Jake hesitated as he thought back to the horrified look on the scientists' faces when he had set the Institute alight. He had made sure they all escaped through the far door, though. He might be many things, but he wasn't a killer. He just hoped Basilisk hadn't seen what he had done.

"Of course I'm not evil," retorted Jake.

"No? You're a warrior. People fear you. You bring much misery to the ordinary folk around you and you enjoy the power, don't you? Power over those scared kids in school; power over your sister." Jake glanced askance at him: so he knew he had a sister. How much more did this creep know about him? "Power over those scientists' lives."

Jake had to admit, it did feel good.

"Power is what Villain.net is all about. I have ambitions to rule the world, shape it in my image. But so did Napoleon, and that did not make him bad."

"So did Hitler," answered Jake, thankful that *some* of his history lessons had sunk in.

"But at the time many saw Hitler as a hero, the man who would revive Germany. They never saw the darker side until it was too late. History is shaped by the winners, never the losers."

Something occurred to Jake. "So are there super-heroes too?"

Basilisk growled derisively. "According to the authorities, yes. The Invisible Brigade among them, so-called goodies even though they will stop at nothing to get what they want either. But they do it under the banner of 'law and order.'" Basilisk thumped the dashboard with his fist, his knuckles leaving an indent.

"And these heroes have the same powers?"

"Similar powers, not quite the same. They want to shape the world in their own image just as much as we do. There is an old saying: Who polices the police?"

That made logical sense to Jake. But before he could flip the thought around, Basilisk continued.

"You have proved that your potential is vast."

Once again Jake felt an unexpected surge of pride. He was beginning to regard Basilisk in a different light. He understood his thirst for power. That thirst, on a much smaller scale, was what normally propelled Jake through each day.

"So who were you before you became Basilisk? Surely you had a real name?"

Basilisk turned his shadowed gaze on Jake for a moment as though contemplating telling him. "I was once Scott Baker, from Canberra, Australia. I was in the army

and had an accident that triggered my latent powers."
Basilisk said it as though he was reading from a script.

That seemed to be all the biography Jake was getting
for the moment. He thought about the fact that Basilisk
didn't have an Australian accent, but decided not to
bring it up. He looked out of the window; it was once
again dark outside. "Where are we going now?"

"You are going home, as we agreed."

"Home? Why?" Just his luck. The moment he found
something fun to do, something happened to end it. "I
want to stay with you!"

"You will see me again in a couple of days, rest
assured. But for now we cannot raise suspicions. If you
stay away from home for too long, then your parents
will call the police. That is something we dare not risk
at the start of an operation."

"But I don't even know what the operation is! You
haven't told me."

"At the moment, the less you know the better. It's
for security. Believe me, even now some do-gooder will
be probing around the technology institute we just
destroyed, looking for clues. Fortunately, with no sur-
vivors, they will have little to go on."

Jake remained silent, and stared at the floor. He
could sense Basilisk briefly turn to look at him. Did he
know what Jake had done? Was this a test?

"So what's next?" said Jake, eager to change the subject.

"I shall return to my base and prepare the Probe. In the meantime, you rest. There will be much for you to do when my plan rolls into operation."

Jake sighed and decided to press again. "What is the plan?"

"All in due time, Hunter. You will know soon enough."

It was almost five in the morning by the time Jake was dropped back at the steel mill and it was still dark. The SkyKar had flown so quickly that the dawn light in India had yet to cross through time zones to reach him. A thin layer of frost had coated his bicycle but at least it hadn't been stolen.

Jake's gaze combed the star-spangled sky. He was no longer feeling frightened by being left alone in the factory, but instead curious as to why Basilisk had chosen him. Clearly he'd been spied on, but for how long? And what was all that stuff about it being "in his blood?"

So far Jake had had no clear goals in his life, or role models to follow. But now he did. He wanted to be like Basilisk—he wanted the freedom to do as he wished and he wanted power—power over people so they wouldn't hassle him anymore.

Feeling good, Jake pedaled furiously home. For once he knew how he wanted his life to play out. And it was full of exciting possibilities.

Grand Designs

* * *

Something roused Jake from sleep. His blurry vision gave way to the digital red numbers on his alarm clock informing him that it was a little after midday.

Jake still felt tired as he went downstairs, even though he had fallen asleep the moment his head had touched the pillow. Vivid dreams had replayed the events in India—the faces of the terrified scientists staring at him, pleading for their lives. And his dreams created bizarre images of him and Basilisk riding the Core Probe to the center of the earth like a motorcycle, heading for some unknown destination, before it melted from the intense heat.

His family was already around the kitchen table having lunch. Jake slumped into his seat as his parents mumbled their "good mornings" or rather, their "good afternoons." His sister looked at him across the table.

"What're you staring at?" he growled.

"You look terrible, Jacob."

"So do you," he snapped back.

His mother studied him, concern on her face. "You do seem a little pale, hon." She touched his forehead. "Temperature's fine though."

"There's nothing wrong with me." Although in truth he did feel weak. Perhaps that was a side effect of last night's exertion?

"You hungry? I'm making grilled cheese."

"Fine," Jake said, turning his attention back to his sister.

"It'd be hysterical if you were sick during the holidays," she said with a thin smile.

"Shut up."

His dad intervened without taking his eyes from the crossword he had been attempting to complete. "Jake, don't tell your sister to shut up."

Beth looked triumphant as she shoveled a spoonful of soup into her mouth. "I think you should stay locked in your room until we're back at school. In case it's contagious. I wouldn't want to catch *anything* off *you*."

Jake's temper snapped and he jumped to his feet, stretching his hand toward his sister, willing a stab of radioactive energy to hurl her off her seat.

Nothing happened.

He tried again, but succeeded only in making his sister stop eating. She frowned. "What are you doing? Got a cramp in your hand?"

"I'm trying to melt your spoon!" he snarled, puzzled.

"You are seriously weird. I hope that's not genetic."

Jake realized he must look like a fool, poised over the table in an action stance, but he had other things to worry about. His superpowers were completely gone.

"Congratulations for activating your account," Jake read.

Grand Designs

As soon as lunch was over, he'd dashed to his room and logged onto his e-mail. "Your continued membership has been approved by the Council and a Villain.net representative will once again be in touch with you to further your new career."

Jake felt a thrill. At least that meant the adventure wasn't over yet. He was about to close the e-mail when a rider at the bottom of the message got his attention. "Villain.net is not responsible for injury, damage, or death to either the End User (yourself) or others (victims) due to utilizing online powers. Any criminal use will be approved and endorsed on condition that Villain.net receives a ten percent commission from all monetary gains."

Jake went back on the Web site in the hope that he could still download the powers and experiment with them on his own. A message in the center of the screen read "SERVICE RUNNING" and prevented him from clicking any of the options. Jake was disappointed. How long would he have to wait to experience that power again?

He shut down the computer and crossed to his window. Outside it was a gloriously chilly day. He glanced at the mirror on his wall, which was almost concealed by stickers and postcards he'd amassed, and ran a hand across his face. He did seem a little paler than usual.

Jake decided he should get something to eat and then

maybe find his gang around town. At least that would give him something to do rather than just sit and wait.

The week slowly crawled by without any word from Basilisk. Jake began to obsessively check his e-mail. His elation at finding a new message was shattered when it turned out to be from Big Tony, with a short abusive paragraph, which Big Tony had no doubt found hilarious when he wrote it.

One day, out of curiosity, Jake typed "Basilisk" into a search engine and chose one of the first of the two and a half million hits, which was a link to Wikipedia. The entry explained that the basilisk was a mythical creature whose gaze could kill. Jake wondered if Basilisk had named himself or if it was a nickname given by others.

Jake longed to tell his friends about his experience, but knew they would accuse him of lying, and no doubt it would all end in a fight. Another side of Jake whispered selfish thoughts: this was a gift for *him*, not them.

His ambivalence toward the gang must have started showing. Scuffer pulled Jake aside to have a whispered conversation as they walked back from yet another knuckleheaded expedition to a street corner.

"You feelin' all right?" Scuffer asked, his eyes constantly twitching as though he couldn't focus on one thing.

"Yeah, why?"

"Well, I know this sounds a bit . . . weird . . . you know, but you're lookin' white like a ghost. Not turnin' into a Goth, are ya?"

"Just not sleeping enough," Jake replied casually. But in fact he had noticed that. His face was normally pink and healthy, but dark bags had slowly appeared under his eyes even though he had slept longer than usual.

"And you don't seem to be havin' fun no more."

Jake glanced at him, and concealed a smile. Could it be that this band of roughneck thugs was actually worried that their faithful leader was losing interest in them?

"You know how it is. I've just been thinking about things. That's all."

"Like what?"

"Just stuff," Jake replied, deliberately ambiguous. From the corner of his eyes he saw Scuffer glance at him, but he didn't say anything else.

By Thursday, Jake had decided not to meet his friends at their regular rendezvous and sent them a text message to cancel. He was sure they would react aggressively and he turned off his phone so he couldn't receive the barrage of replies from the three of them. Besides, he had something else to think about. After checking his e-mail for what must have been the tenth time that morning, he had received one simple message from Villain.net. Just two words: "SERVICES REQUIRED."

Jake waited in his room for further instructions. Outside, the fine day had become stormy. Torrential rain pelted the windows and lightning forked overhead. Jake watched the light show from his window. He loved thunderstorms, in direct contrast to his sister, who was always frightened by them and preferred to hide in her closet until they passed.

He suddenly became aware that somebody was standing just beyond the toolshed at the bottom of the garden, hidden by the trees. Another flash of lightning did little to illuminate the figure. But Jake was sure he knew who it was.

"Basilisk!" Jake grabbed his scuffed black leather jacket from the floor, and climbed out of the window. He ran across the waterlogged lawn, and the figure moved farther back into the trees that separated Jake's yard from a field.

Jake pushed away the branches, and then saw the SkyKar on the edge of the field. Basilisk, sitting inside, motioned him over. Jake was delighted and sprinted to the vehicle.

"Quickly, we have much to do," Basilisk said with a sense of urgency. Jake saw him scrutinize a monitor showing a radar display of what he presumed was the immediate area.

Grand Designs

"Good to see you too," Jake said with heavy sarcasm. This time he buckled himself firmly in the seat as the gull-wing doors closed on them with a pressurized hiss.

The SkyKar lifted from the ground and shot off toward the clouds as lightning flared again.

A damp figure watched from the trees. He'd managed to attract Jake's attention when he had seen him at his bedroom window, and had been planning on leaping out to frighten him.

Only when Jake had run past did he notice the strange vehicle sitting in the field. He'd watched Jake climb in and stood with an open mouth as the craft vanished into the clouds.

Scuffer gawked at the sky in amazement, only blinking when the rain stung his eyes. What had Jake gotten himself involved in?

The SkyKar shook as it passed through the turbulent clouds, forcing Jake to grip the door to brace himself. Rain spattered across the windshield. Jake flinched when he saw a finger of lightning poke from the black clouds above and strike the SkyKar.

"Watch out!" he screamed as he shut his eyes. He could still see the lightning afterimage temporarily burned on his retina.

"It's okay, we're not grounded," explained Basilisk.

"Lightning strikes airplanes all the time, and harmlessly passes through until it hits the ground."

Jake looked through a break in the clouds, down at the houses below him, and wondered what the lightning had struck after it had been diverted by the SkyKar. He believed he could see a set of telephone wires flare up as lightning struck them, the electricity channeling toward a house that had a large oak tree in the yard. Someone probably just had their phones blown out, and their modem too if they had a computer.

He was shoved back into his seat as the SkyKar jolted. They passed through more clouds and then emerged into suddenly clear blue skies. They must be high, as from here he could just make out the gentle curvature of the earth below him. It gave him a slightly sick feeling, like looking through a goldfish bowl.

"I thought I would've heard from you sooner," said Jake, uncomfortably aware that he sounded as reproachful as his mother could when he was in trouble.

"I've been busy," snapped Basilisk. He glanced in Jake's direction, and Jake wondered what lay inside the blackness of the cowl. "It turned out you did not tie up our loose ends in India, and decided to leave some witnesses."

Jake felt butterflies in his stomach, but he managed to keep his face blank. Lying was a superpower of his very own. "They must have escaped. I was sure I locked the door."

Grand Designs

"Whatever happened, it brought the attention of a sneaky superhero who thought he could stop me."

"What happened to him?"

"Ashes to ashes," Basilisk said laconically. Jake shuddered, remembering how Basilisk's gaze had crumpled the scientist to dust. "But there are more on their way. One of whom has a personal vendetta against me."

"Vendetta?"

"I killed his sidekick in a previous encounter. It seems he was rather attached to her."

Jake looked out of the window and saw they were already over the sea. He tried not to think about what had happened, but the question was already on his lips. "Why did you kill her?"

"If she had wanted to live, all she had to do was stop meddling. Very few people, even with superpowers, can survive having a bomb strapped to them."

At that precise moment an alarm sounded in the cockpit.

"Missile lock," warned a smooth voice from the console.

Basilisk jinked the SkyKar to port so suddenly that Jake's head banged against the side window.

"What's happening?" said Jake—but as soon as he asked, the entire SkyKar shook as a military jet fighter shot overhead, its afterburners spluttering out as it circled around. Jake had no idea what type of aircraft it was, but it looked deadly.

"Enforcers!"

"Who?"

"They're like an international antisuperpower police unit."

"How did they know where we'd be?"

"They've been on our tail since your failure in India. The witnesses recognized your voice and ID'd us. They probably picked up the SkyKar's radar signature as I entered their airspace."

"Unidentified aircraft," crackled a voice over the Sky-Kar's radio. "You are in restricted airspace. Turn away from your current flight path and follow us."

Jake noticed another sleek aircraft to their side, the copilot waving his hand to signal they should land. "Can we outrun them?"

Basilisk keyed something on his computer. Seconds later the HUD showed schematics of the aircraft that were intercepting them. Typhoon fighters, more commonly known as the Eurofighter: one of the most advanced fighting planes in the skies.

"We can, but the SkyKar picks up speed gradually. So while we can outrun them eventually, we can't accelerate fast enough to do it. They'll blow us out of the sky."

The other Typhoon had now circled around to fly on the far side of the SkyKar. Jake looked between the two aircraft, both brimming with weapons.

Grand Designs

"This is what happens if you leave loose ends, Hunter. But we can do something they can't. Hold tight."

Jake anticipated a sudden acrobatic maneuver, but instead Basilisk hit the air brakes. The effect was instantaneous. As the SkyKar ground to a halt the two Typhoons shot past like bullets and had to split apart in order to turn around. As agile as the Eurofighter was, it couldn't hover. Jake spotted the flaw in Basilisk's plan.

"Now we're sitting ducks! They can blow us out of the sky!"

As if the attacking pilots were reading his mind, Jake saw a flash from under the wing of one fighter. Basilisk's computer rang the alarm in its unnervingly monotonous voice.

"Missile launch detected."

The HUD informed them that it was an Aim-9 Sidewinder missile arcing toward them, leaving a candyfloss vapor trail.

"It's gonna hit us!" he yelled unnecessarily.

Basilisk poised one hand over a control and watched the missile zeroing in. At the very last second he mashed the control with his fist and the SkyKar bolted vertically in the air. Jake thought he was on some diabolical carnival ride as he was crushed into his seat. He felt light-headed as the g-forces pooled the blood to his legs. When they stopped, Jake saw the missile had overshot, but was circling around on another attack run.

Basilisk edged the SkyKar forward and hit an option on the computer screen. Jake craned around to see a series of brightly colored flares jettison from the SkyKar. They fell to earth away from the SkyKar, and he watched with growing excitement as the heat-seeking missile altered course and homed in to the hottest targets and exploded.

"*Bam!* You got it!" Jake hammered the dashboard in his excitement.

"It won't take long for them to line up another shot," grunted Basilisk as the two Typhoons scissored past in front of them. "We have to fight."

Jake looked at him expectantly. "What kind of weapons has this thing got?"

"Just you," Basilisk said as he reached across Jake and opened the door with a hiss. Cold air flooded the car, and Jake felt his ears pop from the sudden change in pressure.

"Are you crazy?" he screamed as he saw the ocean glittering a long way down, through wispy clouds. He felt a sudden attack of vertigo and pressed himself firmly back in his seat. "No way."

"Remember the Institute? You know I have no weapons for situations like this. You have to—or we both die. And it was your carelessness that got us into this fight!"

Jake stared at the madman, a thousand reasons why he should not leave the SkyKar rattling through his mind. But he realized Basilisk was right. He was their only hope. He gritted his teeth, unfastened his belt, and grabbed the doorjamb to heave himself out.

Jake felt Basilisk suddenly yank him back into his seat.

"You better download some powers before you go!" He angled the monitor for Jake to look at the range of icons on Villain.net. He thoughtfully selected several options.

"No rush," Basilisk said sarcastically.

A sound like fireworks dragged their attention back to the situation outside. One Typhoon was rushing toward them; a Mauser BK-27 cannon was spitting bullets. Jake could see green tracer fire streak past them before the aircraft shot overhead—the slipstream savagely rocking the SkyKar and forcing Jake's finger onto the wrong option.

"Go get 'em!" Basilisk encouraged. "They'll be circling around for another attack run." Basilisk pushed him toward the door.

Jake gripped the doorjamb like a snail. "I don't think I downloaded flying!"

"I told you to be careful!"

"My finger slipped!" Jake snapped back. His fear was more than enough to trigger the powers flowing through his body. "You better keep this thing steady!"

"Get on the roof then and shoot them down!"

"Are you crazy?"

"Hunter! *Now!*"

Jake steeled himself and edged to the door, refusing to look down. His legs felt weak as he reached across and pulled himself onto the hood.

Moving with agonizing slowness, Jake looked around and had to shield his eyes from the sun. He saw one of the Typhoons had turned to face him, its narrow profile making it difficult to see head-on. He heard the SkyKar's computer warn of another missile lock.

"Come on!" Jake yelled defiantly as he raised his hands. He felt small and vulnerable perched on the hood, thousands of feet up, but felt the reassuring swell of superpowers inside. The fighter grew closer, and at such speed it would be on him in seconds. He raised his hands and fired.

A terrible pain shot through his body, and with a crackling sound he saw his arms and legs extend, and his face ached as if he had been punched.

Basilisk watched Jake flail on the hood, and saw the boy's appearance change. He let out a deep sigh; Jake had downloaded a shape-shifting power. He had transformed into a hideous nondescript person, a side effect of trying to change without knowing *what* you want to look like.

The Typhoon shot overhead, causing the SkyKar to rock. Jake threw his arms out for support as he slid over the smooth carbon fiber body, dangerously close to the edge. His own features snapped back painfully.

The pilot must have noticed the mutant figure on the hovering aircraft and was stunned enough not to fire. But the second Typhoon didn't seem to have that problem.

"Missile launch detected."

Jake tried to sit upright—just as the SkyKar shot vertically up once more to avoid the heat seeker that narrowly skimmed beneath them.

Jake was pressed flat against the hood from the sudden acceleration and couldn't move. His ears popped painfully—and then Basilisk stopped the ascent.

But Jake kept rising.

Momentum flipped him off the hood like a pancake. He screamed in horror as he soared several feet above the aircraft, which looked like a small toy below him. Then he reached his zenith, arms and legs frantically scrambling in the air like a cartoon character—before plummeting back toward the SkyKar.

The vehicle looked too small a target to hit. But in a second it consumed Jake's vision and he slammed onto the roof, causing the entire aircraft to wobble. He rolled on impact, and the open gull-wing door saved him from falling off the edge.

Jake sat up, rubbing his stinging ribs. He saw the missile had failed to lock onto the flares Basilisk had deployed,

and was heading straight for them. Jake didn't think—he just raised his hands and hoped.

Something sprang from his fingers. It looked like liquid glass and it struck its target—the missile suddenly froze in the air, as if Jake had pressed "pause." Then it dropped like a rock.

Jake didn't have time to gloat as tracer fire sliced by six feet away, the bullets screaming. He spun around to see a Typhoon blasting toward him. He opened his mouth and screamed.

Jake felt his teeth jangle as he emitted an unearthly howl. The sky shimmered from the sonic blast waves that came out of his mouth. They shredded portions of the Typhoon's thin fuselage and ripped a wing off.

Jake ducked as the fighter shot overhead, spiraling out of control. It fell toward the sea. The canopy flew off and the two pilots ejected. Jake watched, transfixed, as the ejector seats shot away from the stricken fighter and parachutes deployed.

"Jake!" came Basilisk's muffled voice. "Stop messing about and hurry up!"

Jake glowered. He was doing his best.

He turned back as the surviving Typhoon lost altitude and passed beneath them, afterburners booming. It took a few moments for him to realize that the aircraft was retreating back to the mainland. Jake boldly swung back through the gull-wing door, the rush of adrenaline making him oblivious to the fifteen-thousand-foot drop beneath him. He yanked the door closed.

"What happened?"

"They're freaking out. They probably don't want to risk losing another fighter. We need to get out of here while we can."

Jake felt sick. "If they're on to us, does that mean they know who I am?"

"Hopefully not yet."

Not yet? The words were not very comforting. Jake felt a rare pang of concern for his family. Were they safe? What would happen to them if the authorities found out who he was? Perhaps he should get out of this situation before it got any worse.

As the SkyKar accelerated Jake figured now was not the time to express his doubts. He quickly fastened his seat belt. "Where are we going now?"

"Stage two."

Several hours later the clouds had vanished to reveal a deep blue ocean as the SkyKar started to descend.

"One of the perks of the job is having an impressive office. Behold, my island."

Basilisk dipped the nose of the SkyKar so Jake could see. Sparkling turquoise water filled the horizon. Straight ahead was an island covered in verdant jungle and fringed by pure white-sand beaches. At the center of the island sat a steep volcano, blowing thin black vapors that caught the gentle breeze.

Jake grinned. "That's so cool! Where are we?"

"The Pacific Ocean."

"And you own this island?"

"Every inch. My base is deep beneath the volcano. See the entrance?"

Jake noticed a circular metal platform poking from the jungle at the bottom of the volcano, held aloft on a hydraulic pole so it resembled a waiter's arm holding a serving tray.

Basilisk skillfully landed the SkyKar without the slightest bump and opened the doors. Jake could feel the tropical air rush into the cockpit, and he started to sweat under his thick leather jacket. A rich, fragrant aroma hit his nostrils, and a cacophony of birdsong whistled through the air. Before he could take it all in, the platform plummeted underground. Black walls immediately replaced his view. Jake looked up to see the circular portal of daylight grow smaller by the second.

The chute gave way to a spacious cavern, and they came to a smooth halt. Several circular doorways radiated from the cavern like the points on a compass. The stolen Core Probe rested on a steel framework in the center of the chamber, connected to banks of computers. Tools and workbenches were strewn everywhere, giving the appearance of a disorganized garage. Dozens of thick power cables snaked across the bare rock walls and domed ceiling, powering suspended floodlights. There was nothing else in the room, and Jake had the feeling that the base had only recently, and hastily, been constructed.

Basilisk spread his arms and boomed enthusiastically. "And here we are! What do you think?" His voice echoed from the rough stone walls.

"Uh, good?" Jake was feeling disappointed. He had expected more teams of people running around, computers, and other paraphernalia. All brand new and squeaky clean.

Basilisk picked up on his unimpressed tone. "We're a quarter of a mile below an active volcano, on my own private island! What does it take to impress kids today?"

"I was just expecting more people."

"I have a skeleton staff running this joint. People cost money, boy! And that's what we need right now."

"You said you didn't want money," said Jake, who was always reluctant to part with his cash.

"I said I didn't want *your* money. And I also said that this is stage two. You're going to help me get rich. 'Us' rich, I mean," he added hastily.

Jake followed Basilisk through one of the doors, which rotated open with a faint *schnickt* sound, like a camera iris. It led to an equally unimpressive passageway forty

feet long that was hewn from the rock and ended in another circular door.

The next room was slightly more impressive. It was roughly the size of Jake's house, with a massive screen mounted on the wall showing multiple camera views across the island. More cables ran across the floor to dozens of computers on desks so new that the cardboard packaging was still propped against the wall. Six technicians, wearing white coveralls with their regular clothes underneath, sat at the terminals. They all looked up respectfully as their boss entered.

"Satisfied?" Basilisk asked sarcastically.

"It's better. I guess you haven't had the place very long?"

"Less than a month. Now pay attention to the screen." The island views gave way to a live satellite image of the earth. "To rule, you must have power and money, and to get money you need leverage. And a command center like this," he gestured to the room around him.

"What do you mean by leverage?"

"Leverage is something you use to threaten people to get your way."

"Like threatening to punch some kid if he doesn't hand over his lunch money?" asked Jake, drawing from his own real-life example.

"Exactly. Except countries tend to be a little mean about handing over their lunch money, unless you threaten more than one of them. Like the entire world, for example."

A flat map replaced the satellite image. A flashing blip indicated their location just below the equator in the Pacific Ocean. From the amateur quality of the graphics, Jake could tell they were created cheaply. But he kept quiet.

"We have the Core Probe, and with it the power to pierce the earth's heart." The computer graphics abruptly changed to a cutaway view of the earth, and the blinking dot traveled slowly through the different layers of the earth, toward the core. Basilisk narrated its path. "Through the lithosphere, the asthenosphere, and into the mesosphere. Then it will explode, creating a worldwide catastrophe." A chill ran down Jake's spine at the thought, but he was too fascinated to raise any moral objections. "Leverage. We will be able to demand whatever we want!"

"The Core Probe can do that?"

"With a little assistance, yes."

"What would happen?"

"The earth would tilt from its axis. A change of axis would alter seasons, affect the ocean currents, and cause droughts. Doing what global warming couldn't achieve in a thousand years. *That* is leverage."

"But that's crazy!"

Basilisk barked with laughter. "Exactly! That's why it

will work. Of course, the world's governments will try our hand and force us to launch the device. Blah, blah, blah. But, as usual, at the last moment they will concede and give in to our demands. We deactivate the machine, get rich, and everybody's happy." He snapped his fingers like a showman.

"So what are you waiting for?"

"By itself the Probe can't tilt the earth. We need to load it with explosives and then set them off at the core."

Jake guessed the next part. "But you don't have the explosives."

"No, or the money to buy what I need. So we're forced to resort to pettier crimes to achieve a grander scheme. But it provides a perfect training opportunity for you."

"What am I going to do?"

"A little blackmail. *You* are going to perform a kidnapping."

Jake's stomach jolted with a sick feeling as he guessed that things were about to get very messy. For the first time since they had arrived at the base, Jake's thoughts strayed back to his family, and the Enforcers who were pursuing him.

"I need time to think about this."

"There is no time to think, Hunter."

Jake found a vacant seat and dropped into it. The

reality of the situation was just occurring to him. "If those Enforcer guys tracked me to where I live, then what if they get my family?"

Basilisk paused, as though searching for the right argument to convince Jake. "What has your family ever done for you?"

Jake opened his mouth to answer. They had very little direct contact with him, but then the freedom he had was a gift of sorts.

"The Enforcers don't yet know where you live, otherwise they would have picked you up before I could. You're safe from them for now. But when they do find you, you better have something to use against them."

Jake couldn't help but notice that Basilisk's comments were about him directly—he never said "*us*." But he had to admit that Basilisk had a point. It was a big country, and the only time he had used his powers was at school. And that had been an accident.

Basilisk softened a little. "I am aware that killing does not appear to be your style. At least not at the moment. Rest assured that there is nothing harmful in what you're about to do. Look." The screen changed to a surveillance picture of a middle-aged man entering a gallery. "He's a wealthy businessman, with a few million to spare. All you have to do is bring him back here. Alive. Think you can do it?"

Jake's mouth was dry as he stared at the screen, but he nodded wordlessly.

"Good. Let's get you some different powers then. And remember: if he does give you any trouble, knock him out, because he's sure to try and kill you first."

Jake took a deep breath. How much more trouble could he possibly get into?

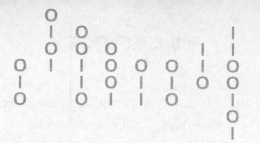

Kidnapped

The life of a supervillain was not shaping up quite the way Jake had imagined. Basilisk had instructed him to contact his parents to tell them he'd be staying over at a friend's house. Hardly a clandestine supervillain activity, but Basilisk insisted it was important to maintain a normal appearance and create an alibi. Secretly, Jake was relieved to have the opportunity to check that the Enforcers hadn't threatened his family. He got through to his parents' answering machine and left a vague message. But he was glad he didn't have to explain himself further.

He spent the rest of the day skimming through surveillance photographs of the gallery owner he had been tasked to abduct: Karl Ramius, a Ukrainian businessman who dealt in fine antiquities and art, and who owned a gallery in the city close to Jake's hometown.

Jake's initial apprehension at the notion of kidnapping evaporated when Basilisk explained that most of the Ukrainian's fortune was made from drug smuggling, and that he laundered the money through the gallery so that

VILL@IN.NET

it appeared to be legally obtained. Ramius was estimated to be worth forty million dollars, and Basilisk anticipated a modest two million ransom would suffice.

Later, Jake rested in a small room that was no larger than the shed back home, but at least it had new furnishings. So new that he had to pull the Bubble Wrap off the bed himself.

Although he was exhausted he couldn't sleep right away. He thought about his family, and the fact that he never had bothered trying to spend time with them. He shook off the thoughts and chalked them up to a rare bout of homesickness. Then his attention turned to Lorna, the girl at school. She'd been nice to him when others usually kept their distance, but rather than talk to her all he'd done was mumble embarrassingly. He sighed deeply and wondered why he always managed to mess things up.

After a fitful sleep he was given a laptop to browse through Villain.net and select powers that appealed to him. Some of the stick figures were indecipherable: one had straight lines coming from its head, another jagged lines, while others had wavy lines, and then all three were repeated in various combinations with Morse-code–like dots and dashes. Basilisk had indicated the icon representing flying, although to Jake it looked as if the figure had just fallen flat on its face. Jake selected that, and another three that looked menacing enough.

Kidnapped

After he had chosen four powers, the unnerving mercury finger curved out and tapped his forehead.

He glanced at his watch and noticed it was almost time to commence the operation. When he arrived at the city it would be Saturday afternoon, and Ramius would be closing the gallery, an ideal time to strike. Jake returned to the command center to find Basilisk in discussion with another caped weirdo.

The newcomer was tall and muscular, wearing a gray and black outfit with a curious whirlwind logo on his chest, and a black flowing cape. What was most unusual was the man's head. It was bucket shaped, with a high sloping forehead and pale skin that was almost translucent, showing the blue veins beneath. A mop of greasy black hair crowned his head. Jake overheard Basilisk refer to him as Doc Tempest.

"It's a good thing you broke away when you did," said Doc Tempest. Jake thought he looked nervous, his hands fidgeting with a pair of power-dampening handcuffs.

"The Council has no vision, Tempest. But they won't be a problem much longer, I assure you."

"Good. Um . . . why is that?"

Basilisk's fingers rolled on his desk, making a sound like hailstones. "You will see with the rest of the world. But the Council of Evil will soon be no more."

Jake frowned. Basilisk had mentioned the Council before. Now it appeared he was plotting against it.

Tempest nodded eagerly, and again Jake couldn't shake the feeling that the villain was nervous. "Getting equipment through the Council is proving more difficult every day. Chromosome is having a hard time getting new biotech gear for her Legion, and she's *on* the Council. The paperwork is crazy. I need more glider-discs too. It's a bigger operation than I—" Alerted by a sixth sense, Tempest suddenly whirled around to face Jake. "Who is this sneaking around?"

Jake's gaze was glued to the newcomer's enormous forehead, blue veins wriggling like worms. "What happened to your head?"

Tempest glowered back, subconsciously running a hand through his lank hair. "I fell into a vat of chemical dry ice when I was a child. It gave me extraordinary powers." He raised his fist; ice suddenly cracked across his glove as the air around it super-chilled. As soon as he unclenched his fist, the ice vanished and Tempest flashed his jagged teeth at Jake, obviously pleased with the chance to show off.

Basilisk leaned back in his chair and steepled his fingers as he fixed his hooded gaze on Tempest. "You still owe me money for the satellite service on that Storm Engine of yours."

"I've had a few minor cash-flow problems caused by four little brats from that stupid dot-com site. The sooner somebody shuts it down the better!"

"Maybe you should take a hostage? Always stops meddlers."

Tempest looked thoughtful. "You think so? Never really been my style. You've got to feed them, clothe them, make sure the doors are locked . . . just seems like a lot of hassle."

Basilisk shrugged. "I find family members are always good leverage for situations like yours."

Jake couldn't shake the feeling that Basilisk was looking at him when he said this. But the dark hood meant he couldn't be sure.

Tempest brightened. "Maybe you're right. I'll grab their mommy. That'll put the little beggars in their place!" Tempest stood and swirled his cape theatrically. "Until next time!" He walked from the room without giving Jake another glance.

"Who was that psycho?"

"He calls himself Doc Tempest. Not the brightest of villains. He's built some kind of weather machine and still owes me money for launching the satellite that deflects his machine's rays around the globe. He's one of the more theatrical types in our business, into all the old-school cackling and swaggering. He's a very odd character."

"Is he always that nervous?"

Basilisk sounded thoughtful. "No. If I didn't know him better, I would suspect him of betraying me to the Council. But enough of him. Are you ready?"

Jake hesitated. This was his very first solo supervillain mission, a real test of his mettle. He felt the tingle of super-energy trickle through him and knew this was too good an opportunity to miss. Whatever Jake's doubts were, and whatever he had to do, Basilisk was offering a rare chance and he would be a fool to pass it up. He was already tangled in this mess. What did he have to lose?

Jake nodded firmly.

"Good," Basilisk said mirthlessly. "Let's go and extort some money."

The SkyKar was on autopilot for the entire journey, since Jake was traveling alone. It kept low, trying to avoid detection by the various air-traffic controls of the countries he passed over. The rumble of the engines was lulling him to sleep when he noticed a key design fault with the craft: the lack of a radio. The time alone allowed him to examine the chain of events that had brought him here.

Villain.net had been stolen, but from where, from whom, and how it actually worked, remained a mystery. Jake guessed there must be some method of storing superpowers so they could be downloaded in the first place. Did that mean there was a host of supervillains sharing their powers via the Internet, or were the powers all artificially created?

Kidnapped

Basilisk had insinuated there were higher powers at work, and had mentioned "The Council of Evil," but who was on the Council? And why did Basilisk want to bring it down?

The next piece of the puzzle was Basilisk's reasons for kidnapping the gallery owner. He mentioned it was to buy explosives, but what kind of explosives cost a cool two million? And would the governments of the world really give in to blackmail? After all, who was insane enough to really *want* to tilt the world off its axis?

Turbulent thoughts sailed through Jake's mind, and his imagination started to kick in about what *he* would be like as ruler of the world. He'd be able to have anything he wanted, and if it didn't exist, he would have the best scientists at his fingertips to invent it. He could live anywhere he wanted. Somewhere on a tropical beach sounded fantastic.

And he would ask Lorna if she would come and stay for a while. He was surprised by that last thought, but it made sense. She wasn't intimidated by him and seemed to like talking to him. Perfect company.

A soft beeping from the SkyKar woke Jake. He'd drifted asleep with dreams of a mansion on a golden Australian beach and his own private jumbo jet, complete with bowling alley, which would take him anywhere he wanted. Reality overruled the dream. There was a light rain on the canopy above his head, while below lay

drab city streets. The SkyKar was landing on the roof of the Ukrainian's gallery.

Jake climbed out, feeling apprehensive. He fingered a small aerosol can in his pocket. Basilisk told him a single squirt would render the Ukrainian unconscious. Then it occurred to Jake that he wasn't wearing any kind of disguise. His face wasn't concealed, and his spiky blond hair was distinctive. He had no choice but to take the man by surprise or else risk being identified later. Why hadn't Basilisk warned him about this?

Jake walked to the edge of the building and peered down the ten floors to the pavement below. His brief sleep had done little to refresh him and he felt irritable—but a voice at the back of his head assured him this was a good thing: didn't anger feed his powers? Or did the powers make him feel angry?

The street was deserted, with just a few vehicles parked along it. He closed his eyes, reminded himself he could fly, and took a step off the edge of the building.

He landed on the pavement and quickly looked around to check he hadn't been spotted. Across the street a pile of rags shifted, and like an optical illusion, a homeless man with a bottle in his hands became visible. He stared at Jake with an open mouth. Jake ignored him; a hobo was no threat.

Two doors down, a doorbell jangled as Ramius left his gallery and gave a quick look around. He only saw a teenager walking toward him, head bowed against the rain. He pulled the gallery door tightly closed and turned keys in three separate locks. Then he turned to his Porsche, parked outside—just as Jake shouldered into him.

Ramius was instantly on the defensive; his fingers clutched a small can of pepper spray he kept in his pocket at all times in case anybody dared mug him. Jake was a flurry of movement, extracting his own knockout gas can and thrusting it into the Ukrainian's face—just as Ramius pulled out his.

They both fired at the same time.

Ramius briefly gagged on the gas jetting into his face, then crumpled like a sack of potatoes. The Ukrainian's pepper spray shot wide, but just enough billowed into Jake's face.

Jake felt his eyes sting, as if acid had been dropped into them. The skin on one cheek burned. He clutched his face and dropped to his knees in agony.

For almost a minute he writhed on the floor, the vision slowly returning to one of his heavily watering eyes. He heard shouting, and looked up to see the hobo run into the middle of the road, arms flailing. At first Jake thought he was dancing drunkenly, until he noticed he was flagging down a police car.

"Aw, no," groaned Jake through gritted teeth. "Idiot!"

He stood, still unable to open his right eye. The

police car had stopped, and a pair of uniformed cops climbed out to pacify the vagrant. Jake couldn't hear what was being said, but the homeless man pointed to the top of the building, then to Jake. The policemen obviously must have thought it was the ramblings of a drunk, as they burst out laughing.

Until they spotted Jake, with the gallery owner slumped at his feet.

The officers ran toward Jake, shouting. "Hey! You over there!"

Jake panicked and crouched down, trying to pull the Ukrainian upright. It was difficult, as the man was twice as heavy as he was, and in a fleeting thought Jake wished he'd downloaded super-strength.

"Superpowers, of course!" Jake stood back up and raised his hands toward the cops and concentrated hard. For safety he had downloaded the radioactive power again; it was something he felt proficient in.

Green tendrils shot out of his hands. A pair of fine strands slammed into the two policemen, knocking them to the floor. The main thrust of the energy struck the police car, which briefly glowed, then exploded in a magnificent fireball. The vagrant dived for cover in a doorway as vehicle fragments struck the wall around him, shattering several windows and triggering car alarms along the street.

Jake bent back down and hooked the Ukrainian's arm

around his shoulder. He hoped that his flying power was going to be able to lift them both. Exerting every muscle in his legs, Jake tried to jump from a crouching position. He shouldn't have worried. He shot into the air like a firework, gripping his hostage tightly so he wouldn't fall.

The cops watched with open mouths as Jake carried the man ten stories up, disappearing on the rooftop. They scrambled for their radios to report the situation.

Jake landed on the roof with a gasp. The higher he had climbed with Ramius, the harder it had been to fly. Obviously there were some weight restrictions with the power. Jake dragged the gallery owner the rest of the way to the SkyKar. Already he could feel the muscles in his arms, legs, and back screaming out as he strained to lift Ramius into the vehicle. He locked the Ukrainian's belt before hesitating. Ramius looked wan, and didn't seem to be breathing. Jake panicked and felt for a pulse on his wrist. Not finding one he checked his neck, breathing a sigh of relief as he detected a strong, steady beat. Leaning close he could now hear shallow breathing. The knockout gas must be incredibly strong, and Jake belatedly remembered Basilisk telling him to spray it a good foot away from the victim. He had accidentally given the Ukrainian a huge dose.

A rhythmic thumping got Jake's attention. He looked

around the rooftop with his one good eye, but couldn't see anything amiss.

The noise was getting louder, and Jake suddenly realized what it was. He scanned the sky until he spotted the approaching police helicopter. He ran to the edge of the roof for a better look.

"Oh, great. That's all I need." Below, an uproar of police sirens rose simultaneously, and he could see flickering blue strobes across several streets, all converging on him. After the incident with the jet fighters he had no wish to fight a helicopter.

His bullying instinct told him to run.

He ran back to the SkyKar and jammed the doors closed. All he had to do was remember how to activate the autopilot. He thought back to the hangar on the island. Basilisk had briefed him on the SkyKar's various safety features, but Jake had been staring at the Core Probe as a couple of engineers welded a lattice cradle to the top of it. Jake had wondered what it was for. He only zoned back to Basilisk when the villain had wished him luck and thumbed a button on the touch screen. The autopilot switch!

The helicopter was now circling overhead with a loud clatter of rotors. A hesitant voice boomed over the aircraft's loudspeaker.

"You in the . . . uh . . . car on the roof. Come out with your hands up!"

Kidnapped

Jake examined the multitude of options on the screen. They were all labeled with icons. What was it with these people—couldn't they just spell out what the buttons did? Jake had a feeling Basilisk had touched the button that showed an image of the SkyKar.

Jake pressed it.

The SkyKar whined to life and spoke: "Autopilot engaged."

"Way to go!" he screamed jubilantly.

The vehicle shot up vertically, surprising the helicopter pilot who thrust aside sharply. Jake instinctively pushed himself back in his seat, as the chopper's lethal rotors filled the windshield as he sped past.

Soon they would be in the clouds, and speeding toward safety. The SkyKar suddenly shuddered. Jake heard several heavy thumps against the fuselage as a pair of bullet holes punctured the SkyKar's nose.

They were shooting at him.

"What're you doing?" Jake screamed. He'd watched enough police chase shows on television to know that police helicopters were not supposed to be armed. But he saw the sharpshooter hanging from the side door of the chopper as it banked around.

The rifle was aimed in his direction—until a muzzle flash and a violent thud came from underneath. The computer screen glitched: "You have manual control." The SkyKar stopped ascending, and hovered in the air.

"What? No! I don't want manual control. I want to get out of here!" shouted Jake. The vehicle lurched as he thumped the control stick. He looked up to see the helicopter bearing down on him.

"Land now, or we will shoot you down!" came the voice of the chopper pilot.

"Don't you know I have a hostage? You'll kill us both!" Of course they couldn't hear his panicked cries. He also knew that unless he took the controls he'd be history.

He gripped the control column, and his fingers rested on a set of hand grips and buttons like they'd done many times on his game console at home. His feet found a set of pedals, and he hoped his instincts would get him through this. He tried to recall Basilisk's actions when they had been outmaneuvering the Typhoon fighters.

The SkyKar suddenly jolted low, just underneath the helicopter, which rotated to give chase. It was a skillful move—even though Jake had been attempting to rise *over* the chopper.

"Controls are inverted!" he said through gritted teeth. And, unlike his computer games, Jake doubted there would be an option to reconfigure them.

The ground rose up to greet Jake, and he pulled back hard on the stick. The SkyKar leveled out three feet above the traffic. He zoomed past parked cars, the air pressure setting off their alarms. Three police cars squealed in pursuit, the helicopter thundering just above them.

Jake pulled on the stick, and swung the SkyKar around into another street. He was going so fast he barely made the turn—the underbelly of the vehicle shattered several office windows as he slewed wide, scraping a building. Jake leveled out. The gallery was in a quiet part of the city, but now he had just turned onto one of the main avenues, and the Saturday traffic below squealed to a halt as the drivers and pedestrians watched the SkyKar race overhead.

Below, the police were struggling to keep up. One took the turn wide and crashed into another car whose driver had stopped midway past a crossroads to gape at the flying car.

Jake glanced at the dashboard and saw one button that resembled a camera. He pressed it and the monitor screen turned into a split view of what was behind and below him. He could see the police chopper was hot on his tail. Jake didn't have the expertise to lose the helicopter. He'd have to rely on something else.

He gently released the control stick, and the craft remained steady and straight. The road below was long, so Jake took the chance to open the door and lean out. The air blasted his ears, and caused his good eye to smart. He kept one hand firmly gripping the door frame, twisted himself backward, and leaned as far as he dared to face the pursuing helicopter.

He saw the sharpshooter raise his gun—then hesitate when he realized Jake was only a boy.

A bad mistake.

Jake extended his hand. He was mad at himself for messing up such a simple job; that anger manifested itself in his superpowers.

Millions of tiny pellets issued from Jake's hand, like black ball bearings. They extended into a thick cloud of hail that the copter flew straight into. The effect was instantaneous.

The chopper's windshield shattered, and the rest of the fuselage was peppered with pinholes. The pellets struck through to the engine and instantly caused metal to grind against metal. Black smoke poured from the engine, as fragments of the rotor were torn off.

In seconds, the helicopter dropped from the sky. The damaged rotors slowly revolved as the air forced them to turn, something pilots called autorotation— effectively serving as a parachute and saving the crew inside.

The chopper landed on top of a bus, the roof of which crumpled, tipping the helicopter sidelong onto a taxi. The rotors shattered as they hit the road; people scattered in all directions.

A smile crawled across Jake's face as he watched. "No

way!" He'd broken things before, but nothing on this scale.

He pulled the gull-wing door shut. Catching his breath he thumbed the autopilot button. It didn't respond.

"Come on!" He snarled and irritably punched the dashboard. The autopilot light suddenly flashed on, and the computer confirmed it.

Jake forced himself to relax as the SkyKar sharply angled up and accelerated. His hostage was peacefully slumbering next to him.

He'd done it: his first solo task, and he'd enjoyed it—the suspense, the thrill of the chase, and the ultimate sensation of living on the edge. Jake Hunter was officially a supervillain, and he felt proud.

What he didn't know was that his picture was currently being circulated by police forces across the country, and then passed on to worldwide antiterrorist units. By the time Jake had returned to Basilisk's hideout, he had become the most wanted criminal in the country.

And by the following week, he would be the most wanted supervillain in the *world*.

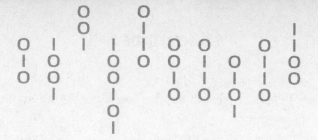

Just Another Day

To say it had been a strange weekend would have been a gross understatement. Jake lay on his bed, in the familiar surroundings of his home. He was feeling restless as he gazed blankly at the ceiling, his mind churning over recent events.

Returning to Basilisk's volcanic paradise had been straightforward. The supervillain had started to ask Jake if the mission went smoothly, but the question drifted from his lips when he saw the bullet holes peppering the SkyKar. The swelling in Jake's eye had faded, and he'd finally got his sight back. Embarrassed, Jake had to tell Basilisk about the police pursuit across the city. Basilisk didn't say a word, but his fists clenched with an audible crunch.

Then Jake was left alone for a while, and he decided to take the opportunity to get some fresh air and explore the island. As he soared up the access tunnel leading to the surface, he could feel the warm tropical air on his face. But as he emerged, the bright sunshine started to hurt his eyes and gave him a headache. His skin felt raw, as though his face had been severely sun-burned. It was a bizarre reaction to a beautiful day, and it forced Jake back underground, wondering if his sister's omen about him falling ill was coming true.

Basilisk strode into the hangar, interrupting his thoughts. "I've issued the ransom demand to Ramius's people, so now we wait. I'm sure they're crooked enough to want to keep this out of the way of law enforcement. If that's possible after half the cops in the country saw you kidnap him!"

"My skin is burning!" Jake said, ignoring Basilisk's accusation.

"Ah, as I feared. You're becoming photosensitive."

"Huh?"

"It means you are becoming sensitive to light. In this case, bright UV rays, like you get from the sun. Don't let it worry you. We're near the equator. The sun is stronger here than anywhere else in the world."

"But why? I never used to be photo . . . whatever."

Basilisk hesitated. "There are occasional side effects from long-term exposure to your superpowers."

Jake scowled. "You said there were no side effects!"

"They're very rare," Basilisk said levelly. "Now, you will return home until phase three."

And so Jake sat aboard the hastily patched-up SkyKar and was ferried home. Basilisk's last words puzzled him during the flight home.

"Keep your head down, and don't mention this to *anyone*. We'll talk soon." He understood that their devious plan was not something he could divulge to friends. But why would he have to keep his head down?

Jake arrived at his house and walked straight into the living room where his parents were watching television. He was about to tell them his preprepared lie about what he'd done with his friends, when his mother shot him a look of concern.

"Jake, do you feel okay?"

"Fine, why?"

"You look very pale. As if you're sick. Have you been sleeping okay?"

Jake assured her that he had been and tried to leave the room, but his eyes strayed to the news.

An anchorman was talking about an attempted bank robbery in the city the day before. The sudden surge in violence across the country had prompted the mobilization of SWAT teams. And it was one such air patrol that had tried to foil a kidnapping. The ensuing car chase had caused chaos, the reporter said, but Jake noticed there was no mention of the fact that his car was *flying*.

Then the image changed to a fuzzy shot of Jake himself. It was a close-up as he hung from the SkyKar, taken from an angle that didn't make it apparent that he had been in midair. Blurred or not, there was no mistaking that it was Jake.

Just Another Day

He felt a sudden streak of terror turn his stomach. His parents watched the report, failing to make the connection with the image on the screen and their son. But Jake was certain that they would any minute.

The anchorman continued to inform the public that the suspect was wanted for *both* the kidnapping and the bank robbery.

"Police consider him armed and dangerous," the newscaster said directly to the camera. Jake felt the man's accusing gaze was boring into him. "Do not approach him, and if you have any information that may lead to his arrest, contact the police as soon as possible. There is a reward."

The telephone rang. Jake's eyes shot to it, but his limbs refused to move. His mother leaned across and picked it up.

"Hello?" she said.

Jake knew this was the moment his parents would discover his secret. The moment his newfound chance in life would slip from his grasp.

But his mother shrieked with laughter down the telephone. It was one of her work friends calling with gossip.

Jake bolted from the room and took refuge in his bed with a growing sense of dread. He kept away from everybody on Sunday and avoided the television and any news Web sites. He regularly checked his e-mail, but there was nothing from Basilisk.

"It's not fair," he thought, being dependent on the villain. Basilisk had already lied to him about side effects, so what else would he do? Jake just didn't trust him.

He could hardly believe that he was looking forward to returning to school the next day. Anything to derail his obsessive thoughts.

Jake tensed when he walked past Patel's newsstand and saw a display with the *New York Times* headline on it, and the blown-up picture of him in the SkyKar. He was now Public Enemy Number One. Jake studied the picture and decided with relief that maybe identifying him wasn't so easy.

Feeling a little more reassured he walked through the school gates. As usual everybody cleared from his path, but this time he was thankful for it. Rain had been falling hard since he woke up, and the air was unseasonably warm. His mother had been rambling on about the crazy weather all morning. He didn't mind getting wet though, as the clouds blocked the sunlight, and his skin didn't tingle as badly.

He almost walked past his gang, who had the Professor pinned against a wall, threatening him. Jake had to laugh. It seemed they were getting interference from another kid, who Jake knew was Lorna's brother, Toby. Toby was somebody Jake always left alone because of

Lorna. It wouldn't look good beating up the brother of a girl he liked. Scuffer looked over and waved, but Jake kept on walking.

"Jake!"

The voice snapped him out of his thoughts. He turned to see Lorna struggling to enter a classroom, her arms filled with books. Her usual bright smile faltered when she saw his face.

"You okay?" she asked.

Jake bit back a snappy reply. She was somebody he wanted to keep as a friend, so instead he gallantly opened the door for her. "I'm just feeling a bit run down. Haven't been sleeping much." Well, at least *that* was true.

Lorna was grateful for the assistance and hesitated as she entered the classroom. "Thanks. I heard about you saving Mr. Falconer. That was a very brave thing to do, especially after what he did to you." She blushed and looked away.

Jake didn't know what to say. If Lorna knew about Mr. Falconer, then the whole school would definitely be talking about it.

"You'll have to tell me about it," she continued. "You know. After school some time?"

Her cheeks were burning now and she glanced behind him. "Your fan club's here. See you around." She slipped into the classroom, and the door swung shut as Jake felt Knuckles's big hands slap him on the shoulders so hard his knees buckled.

"Hey, Hunter, what's up?"

Jake's thoughts jumbled in his head. One minute he was worrying about being a wanted man, and now he was trying to figure out if he'd just been asked out on a date. He could deal with the notoriety, but girls were uncharted territory. He pulled himself together; Lorna was another item on the growing list of things he didn't want his friends knowing about.

"Knucks. Hey, guys."

Scuffer walked alongside him; never one to make direct eye contact, he looked even more shifty than usual. "Where've you been all week?"

"I have the worst luck. As soon as we're not in school, I get ill."

"Is that right?" mumbled Scuffer.

"You look sick," Big Tony said with a trace of concern. "I'm not going to get it, am I? Don't wanna lose my appetite."

"No chance," thought Jake, but tactfully remained silent.

"Is that all?" pressed Scuffer.

Jake paused; his companions walked several steps onward before they noticed he had stopped. A few days away from his friends made him realize what a dull life they led and how much better it had been without their constant dares and immature behavior. Maybe Jake was finally growing up. But he was suspicious of Scuffer's tone. "What do you mean?"

Scuffer gave a forced, humourless smile. "Nothin.' Just meant: is that all? You didn't get up to anythin' else? You know, flyin' around . . . with your family or somethin'?"

Jake narrowed his eyes as he scrutinized his friends. The three of them looked in every direction except his. The school bell rang, breaking the tension.

"Later," Jake said bluntly before he turned and walked away.

Out of earshot, Scuffer confided to the others. "See, he's actin' weird. I told ya, but you don't believe me. *Swear* I saw him get into some sort of flying thingy the other night. Somethin' strange is going on!"

Knuckles laughed. "We heard you before, and you're still mental."

"I don't understand," said Big Tony. "If you think he's an alien, why is he in school?"

Knuckles broke into laughter. "Yeah, Scuff. You're just losing it."

Scuffer winced as they laughed, his cheeks burning red from embarrassment. He hated being the butt of any joke, and he was certain about what he'd seen. There was something strange going on with Jake Hunter, and he was going to find out exactly what it was.

* * *

Jake was on edge all morning, convinced that a teacher or student was going to single him out and accuse him of the kidnapping. But nothing was mentioned. His fear was then overshadowed by his sudden heroic status as word got around that *he* had saved Mr. Falconer. Of course a parallel rumor circulated that *he* had been the cause of the blaze. As the gossip took on a life of its own, Jake noticed people staring at him from whispered huddles, but with looks of curiosity rather than fear. It was as if he had become a celebrity. He wouldn't admit it, but he had a feeling that he would enjoy being famous.

Or infamous.

Later in computer class, Jake reluctantly started the assignment he'd been given, to research how a small local business could grow through e-commerce, when a thought struck him. Basilisk had mentioned that he was originally from Canberra, Australia. Jake tried to remember what he said he'd been called. His fingers drummed the desk as he searched his memory, and when he glanced up he caught Scuffer quickly looking away. Jake angled his monitor so Scuffer couldn't see. His friend tried not to react, but Jake couldn't help but notice the scowl across his face.

Baker, that was it. *Scott Baker*. Jake typed the name and location into Google along with any other keywords that would help him find information: ARMY, ACCI-DENT.

The search engine churned through its immense database in a fraction of a second and returned over a hundred thousand hits. Only one successfully matched all of his keywords "Scott Baker Army Accident." Jake clicked on it.

A scanned newspaper article from the *Canberra Times* showed a picture of a young soldier, in full army uniform. The headline read: LOCAL HERO KILLED IN FREAK ACCIDENT. Jake read more, but the details were sketchy: apparently it had to do with an army supply tanker flipping off the road; the soldier had been crushed underneath. It wasn't of much use to Jake.

"Killed?" murmured Jake. "Something's not right here."

Checking to be sure the teacher was not standing behind him, Jake went back to Google and typed in the keywords "Basilisk supervillain," and hit the enter key. Moments later a handful of hits came up, but they were old news stories with headlines along the lines of: SPATE OF TERRORIST ATTACKS BY MASKED VIGILANTE NAMED BASILISK. The accompanying stories didn't offer much in the way of detail, other than to say the crimes were still unsolved.

Jake was about to close the original article when something caught his attention: its date. Something about that

date was bothering him. He used the browser's "back" button to return to the Scott Baker story. His eye was immediately drawn to the date imprinted at the bottom of the article—Baker died two years *after* the articles mentioning the masked villain Basilisk.

Basilisk was around long before the accident in Australia. The supervillain had lied to Jake again.

Jake knew about identity theft, when one person uses the name and address of another, effectively stealing their identity in order to extort money from credit cards and bank accounts. That's why his father insisted they shred everything before throwing it out. Is that what Basilisk was after when he took the name of a dead man?

Jake stabbed the mouse button to clear the articles from the screen. He was feeling betrayed, although part of him couldn't quite see why. After all, Basilisk was a supervillain—he was *supposed* to lie. But that small betrayal hurt Jake more than he liked to admit.

Jake looked around the classroom and saw a new kid was staring at him. Had he seen what Jake was doing? Jake was getting increasingly paranoid. Even if the boy had seen, it wouldn't mean anything to him. If Jake wasn't careful, then he would be jumping at his own shadow next.

The lunch bell freed Jake from the class, and he was surprised to notice Scuffer disappearing into the crowd without saying a word. That was a welcome relief, as

Just Another Day

Jake didn't feel like conversation right now, he had too much on his mind. Instead of crossing the schoolyard, Jake chose to head for the cafeteria through the network of corridors within the main school building. Nobody ever went that way. It kept him out of the way of gossipers and finger-pointers.

With both students and teachers gone, Jake's footsteps echoed down the long corridor, which was lined with bulletin boards, posters, and half-open classroom doors. The building was old; the white plaster ceiling was heavy with cracks and flickering fluorescent lights.

"Hey, you!" called a voice from behind.

Jake stopped and turned. At the end of the passage stood the new kid from computer class. He was much smaller than Jake, hugged an armful of books defensively, and wore an oddly blank expression.

"What do you want, shorty?" Jake said brusquely. Although he was small, the boy had given Jake pause. Even people who knew him well would normally think twice before calling out to him.

Maybe he wanted an autograph?

The boy started walking fearlessly toward him. "You're Jake Hunter."

It was a statement rather than a question. Jake felt his hackles rise and his eyes narrowed suspiciously. In his pocket he felt his phone vibrate, no doubt Big Tony and the others trying to track him down.

"Who wants to know?" Jake asked, as the kid got closer.

"So, you're Basilisk's latest sidekick?"

At the mention of the name, Jake felt his blood run cold. Then he remembered that the kid had been sitting next to him while he had been searching the Web. That's probably where he got the name.

"Get lost, shrimp," Jake said, turning his back on the kid.

"Oh, I don't think so, Hunter."

Jake stopped in his tracks. The voice had changed into something gruffer and then he heard the books clatter to the floor. His mobile kept silently vibrating in his pocket as he took a deep breath and turned.

The kid was growing taller and thinner. His shirt merged with his body as his torso narrowed and extended. His arms and legs grew longer. Small curved talons poked from elongating fingers. His sneakers became broad reptile feet. The boy's fleshy skin turned mottled and scaly, and his head transformed into something out of a nightmare—saurian, with broad black eyes and a fat swollen tongue that flicked from his mouth. In a matter of seconds, the boy had turned into a six-foot-tall spindly reptile creature hunched forward on two legs, a thin tail snaking out to balance him.

Jake took a step back, his eyes wide. "What the hell are you?"

The lizard-man replied in a voice that sounded as if it had been dragged across sandpaper. "As if you don't know! They call me the Chameleon, and like you I possess certain . . . "—the tongue lashed out—" . . . gifts. And I'm here for you!" Chameleon pointed a slender clawed finger.

"Wait a minute," said Jake, raising his hands and trying to conjure an escape route. "I think we're on the same side."

Chameleon let out a hoarse laugh. "Same side? You mistake my appearance, Hunter. I'm one of the good guys! Both you and Basilisk have led me in a merry dance. I even had to buddy up with the Enforcers to track you down. And they're not a particularly hygienic bunch."

"How did you find me?" Jake gasped. It was a pointless question, but he was playing for time as he glanced around the corridor for something he could use as a weapon.

"The scientists in India gave us a pretty good description, blondie. Basilisk we knew of already. He'd left his calling card, the petrified bodies and dust. Your new friend is very ruthless. He even blew apart my partner when we sabotaged his last plan." Jake's expression must have given away his surprise. "Oh, don't you know? We go a long way back, to when he kidnapped the president's daughter. You should have picked your

company more carefully, Hunter. I've sworn to bring Basilisk down, and since you have helped him, I'll bring you down too.

"We don't know where Basilisk's hiding out at the moment, but when we detected his SkyKar in the airspace here, and then you destroyed an air force fighter, we knew we were on the right track. A little cross-referencing with any unusual news stories, such as a schoolteacher undergoing psychiatric treatment because he claimed his student was glowing when he set a classroom on fire, and I found your school. Then I just had to make sure it was really you. Using a public computer to search for Basilisk was such a clumsy move I could hardly believe my luck."

"You're a regular Sherlock Holmes," snorted Jake.

"Well, here I am. I'm bringing you to justice."

Chameleon took a step forward, claws clicking on the old parquet floor. Jake tensed, then dived through an open classroom door. As Chameleon clattered into the room, Jake scrambled under a table. The desks in this classroom were long and had been pushed together to accommodate group exercises, making little islands across the room.

"Tried to go invisible, have we?" hissed Chameleon as he leaped up on top of a desk, out of Jake's sight.

Jake heard the gentle patter of claws, and the desk above him shifted slightly as Chameleon stood on it. As silently as possible, Jake crawled across a gap between tables, and hid under another group just as a scaly fist smashed through the wood and clawed the air where his head had been moments before.

"I know you're here, Hunter. I can smell your stench!"

Jake's phone vibrated yet again, giving him an idea. In a last act of desperation he could call the police. Nobody had recognized him from the mugshot on the news, so it was worth the risk that the police wouldn't either, and he might get this freak behind bars.

"You can't stay hidden forever, Hunter," intoned Chameleon. It was lucky Chameleon assumed that Jake still had his powers, or else he would have just ripped up every desk until he got to him.

Jake slid out his phone, his thumb already moving to dial the cops. But when he glanced at the display he hesitated—he had received three text messages from Villain.net.

With a shaking hand he opened the first: it was a simple Web link. Jake resisted slapping his forehead to drum out the stupidity; his phone was capable of surfing the Web. Why hadn't he thought of that before?

Trembling, he initiated the link, and the screen flipped to a shrunken version of Villain.net. The icons were too small to clearly make out, but Jake didn't care. He toggled randomly over them and clicked away.

The desk above his head shifted as the hero jumped across. A set of claws appeared on the edge of the desk and Chameleon's inverted head followed. He looked right at Jake, his vertical pupils narrowing gleefully.

"There you are. And fresh out of powers, I guess?"

"Guess again," snarled Jake, thrusting out his palms to fire a volley of, well, *something*. Instead his jaw painfully extended and a black swarm shot from his mouth, straight at Chameleon with a terrible buzz. The stream stopped, and Jake spat lumps from his mouth in disgust. When he looked at Chameleon he felt sick. He'd exhaled a mass of flies, and they were orbiting the lizard, trying to bite his scaly skin. Chameleon's tongue darted out, and in two flicks he had swallowed the entire swarm.

Jake was irate. "What kind of stupid superpower was that?"

"You should take more care in what you pick," Chameleon hissed with delight.

Anger welled in Jake and he felt his palms heat up. He extended them again and hoped. This time a blinding light shot out and crashed into the underside of the desk. Jake just had enough presence of mind to roll aside as the table above him shot toward the ceiling in a trail of fire—Chameleon perched on top, riding it all the way as it ploughed into the tiles before dropping onto a cabinet. Stacks of textbooks spilled on the ground.

Just Another Day

Jake stood as Chameleon groaned, pushing away the charred desk that pinned him. Before Jake could react, Chameleon performed a serpentine flip onto his feet and swayed in front of Jake like a prize boxer.

"Not bad," hissed the lizard, spitting a glob of blood on the floor. "Let me show you something *really* impressive."

Chameleon spun around. His tail whipped out, extending until it coiled around Jake like a boa constrictor. Jake's arms were pinned to his side as the breath was crushed from him. With a powerful flick, Chameleon hoisted Jake off the ground and skittered toward him.

"Just a little tighter and you'll lose consciousness," Chameleon said as he increased his grip, forcing another gasp from Jake. "Don't worry, Hunter. I'm one of the good guys, so I won't butcher you like your boss did my partner."

"Whatever he did to you has nothing to do with me!" Jake pleaded in short breaths.

"I want my revenge. You picked your partner badly, kiddo. There's no way you're getting out of this!"

WHAM! Something heavy connected with the back of Chameleon's head, forcing the lizard to slump forward and release Jake. His tail snapped back to size as he fell to his knees. Jake instantly flexed both hands forward and another blinding jolt of light swept Chameleon off the floor and smashed him powerfully

through the glass window, into the thorny shrubbery outside.

Jake forced air back into his lungs. He looked up at his savior. Scuffer stood with a fire extinguisher in one hand and a dumbfounded look on his face.

"We better get out of here before that thing comes back. Then you have some *major* explainin' to do, dude."

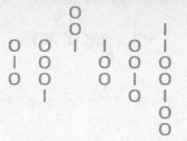

A Plan Unveiled

The dry crack of Knuckles's fist drew Jake out of his reverie. He was standing under the shelter offered by a tree as the rain lashed the boughs. Scuffer, Knuckles, and Big Tony were keeping their distance from him but dared not look away.

"I still don't believe any of this," squeaked Knuckles.

"See if I care," retorted Jake.

Scuffer had ordered the gang out of school and told them what he had witnessed. Jake filled in the gaps, secretly happy, finally, to be able to talk about what had happened. But their questions came pouring out, and he was now beginning to regret opening his mouth. After all, why should they get any fun out of Villain.net?

Then another thought popped into his head. Chameleon knew who he was. That meant the Enforcers would too. Home was no longer safe. How was he going to explain that to his parents? He felt a pang of sadness. All the times he had been sent home from school with bad reports, a suspension, and, on a few occasions, angry parents of the kids he had picked on, he had never felt remorse.

But now he did.

Now he realized that his actions would upset them in a way that was deep and personal. The news would crush them, distressing his parents to a degree he had never seen before. What would they do? Throw him out of the house? Disown him?

"But you're an alien?" Big Tony said in awe.

Jake looked incredulous. The others started to laugh.

"That's what he told me!" blurted Big Tony.

"An alien? That's what you think I am? Do you know how that sounds?"

Scuffer's laughter suddenly evaporated. "About as crazy as you climbin' into a flyin' car or fightin' some kid who transformed into a lizard."

Jake's smile faded. "Guys, trust me. This is not something you want to get involved in."

"Bit late for that, don't you think?" said Scuffer, nervously shifting his weight from one foot to the other.

Jake regarded them all levelly. Then with a sigh, he explained again: "I've already told you. I'm what you call a supervillain." He winced, aware of how lame that sounded. "I downloaded some powers from the Web, and kidnapped that gallery owner . . ." He trailed away.

A Plan Unveiled

Knuckles and Big Tony looked as though they didn't need much convincing.

"That was you?" Big Tony said in awe. "Wow, that bank job—"

Jake was exasperated. "What bank?"

Big Tony blinked in surprise. "The National Bank downtown was robbed the other day. My mom opened an account for me there . . . wait a minute. You didn't rob anything, did ya?"

"No, I didn't! That wasn't me!"

Big Tony looked suspiciously at him. "The crooks blew up half the road, but the cops stopped them from getting away with five million! That's why every city across the country's been on high alert. Helicopters everywhere, armed cops—"

"I just did the kidnapping," snapped Jake. "That is *my* claim to fame!"

Scuffer was silent for a moment as he tried to work things out. "So, that lizard kid, was he a superhero? That why he attacked you?"

Jake shrugged. "Yeah."

"So how many of these superguys are there?"

"Many," boomed a new voice. Everybody whirled around to see Basilisk.

"That's a bizarre costume," said Scuffer.

The eyes beneath Basilisk's hood flared. "You have involved your friends in this, Hunter?"

Jake hesitated. It was as if his dad was reprimanding him. "I had no choice. Scuff here saved . . . uh . . . helped me out when some freak attacked me."

"Chameleon. I heard he was on your trail, trying to track us down. And he did a fine job, I see. Yet again, you left an incompetent mess behind."

"Shut up!" snapped Jake as he raised a finger at Basilisk. "I had enough of that from the freak. I don't need it from you. What I want from you are some answers."

He heard a sharp intake of breath from his gang in anticipation of a fight. Jake half-expected Basilisk to knock him to the floor with a backhand, unleash a power on him, or at the very least shout. Instead he crossed his arms.

"What do you wish to know?"

"You knew Chameleon was closing in on me?"

"That's why I sent the text message to your phone. The powers drawn from that device are not as potent as normal, but it was better than nothing. Otherwise you'd be in Chameleon's hands now."

"And would you have come to spring me?" asked Jake, although he figured he already knew the answer.

Basilisk ignored the question. "Your powers will have faded by now. We're still working out the kinks in using the mobile technology. Luckily, Chameleon is a little new to this modern approach to superpowers. He's what we call a Prime."

A Plan Unveiled

"A Prime?"

"One who possesses his powers naturally, rather than downloading them."

"Just like you. He said he wants you dead."

"Still? He's a fearsome opponent, and I guess he was being gentle with you until he could ascertain just how much of a threat you are. Your next encounter will be far less civilized than that one. But right now, we have more important matters to attend to. Come."

Scuffer stepped forward. "Where can I download these powers from?"

Jake scowled and stepped in front of him. "Wait a minute. What about my family?"

"What about them?"

"If Chameleon tracked me down, then he'll know where I live. I want to make sure he hasn't harmed my family."

"Your family is safe."

"How do you know?"

"The Enforcers do not kill innocent people. Their job includes making sure the public remains unaware of the superpowered. It would not be much of a secret if they talked about it to your parents."

Jake held his ground, unsure whether he should trust him. Basilisk strode forward and gripped Jake's arm. He tried to resist but the villain was just too strong.

"What about them?" Jake asked, gesturing at his crew.

Basilisk cast his gaze among the three silent companions. "They can come too. The next step is a dual mission. If you want company, then why not take some *disposable* assets? Grab ahold of each other."

Scuffer sniggered. "What? Hold hands? What d'you think I am?"

Basilisk loomed menacingly over Scuffer. "Right now you are nothing more than a *henchman*. Grab each other or you will be left behind!"

Big Tony grabbed Knuckles's hand. Knuckles shot him a venomous look and shook him off, instead grabbing Big Tony's shoulder. Jake reached out and gripped Scuffer's shoulder.

"Why are we doing this?"

"They have been tracking the SkyKar so we can no longer use it. We are teleporting to the base."

Seconds before they teleported, Jake thought he saw the storm clouds on the horizon suddenly change direction and drift to form a tornado funnel. He suddenly remembered Doc Tempest and his weather machine just as a thunderclap boomed across the forest, and the five figures vanished in a flicker of light.

A few seconds later they appeared in Basilisk's dark hangar, staggering slightly as a wave of nausea rolled over them. Big Tony couldn't handle it, and dropped to his knees, vomiting against the wall, an act that went on for some time.

Jake quickly looked away, his eyes falling on the Core Probe. The metal cradle on top of the device was complete, and it clearly looked as if something would latch onto it. The bomb, he guessed.

"Follow me," Basilisk said, and strode toward the command center. The others followed, eyes wide, except for Big Tony, who wiped his mouth with his sleeve and trailed at a distance, keeping his eyes firmly on the ground.

"Our ransom demands were met," said Basilisk with a trace of pride. "We have payment, and the Ukrainian was returned to his family." He spun around and Jake sensed Basilisk was staring at him. "Alive and unharmed, before you ask."

"Good," said Jake, and he felt relieved that Basilisk hadn't decided to change the plan. Then he remembered the Ukrainian had seen his face. If he could identify Jake, then he was a threat. Basilisk must have picked up on Jake's thoughts and waved an admonishing finger.

"Mercy will be your weakness, Hunter. It's a useless trait to possess."

"I'll remember that."

They entered the command post, and Jake's three friends gaped around.

"It's like being in a James Bond film!" whispered Big Tony.

"One with a cheap budget," muttered Jake.

"We have two tasks to achieve this afternoon if we are to launch our main operation," said Basilisk.

"What's the main operation, then?" whispered Scuffer.

"I'll tell you later," replied Jake.

Basilisk punched up a satellite view of the world. "The first is in the Persian Gulf. We will rendezvous with an expert on deep-core drilling who has offered his services; at a price, of course." The map changed to an aerial view of an oil platform off the coast of the United Arab Emirates. "It is a simple extraction operation." He turned to glance at Jake. "Or it would have been before you roused the attention of the Enforcers. Now there is the risk that an assault team could be lying in wait."

Jake glowered, embarrassed that Basilisk was showing him up in front of his friends for the second time. "Maybe if I'd been given a little more warning, that wouldn't have happened." He forced himself to relax. "So what do we do?"

"I will deal with them. You and your lackeys have a much more important assignment."

That didn't sound right. After his constant whining about how careless Jake had been, why did Basilisk now trust him with something important? Unless it was another lie, just like the Scott Baker pseudonym.

A Plan Unveiled

Perhaps it was perilous and Basilisk didn't want to risk his own neck? Jake's distrust for the villain increased, and he couldn't shake the feeling that events were well and truly spinning beyond his control.

"You will travel to Moscow, Russia. Red Square, to be precise, and meet this man."

He scrolled the satellite map north, centering on Moscow. A number of photographs appeared on the side of the screen. They were of the same man, taken in different locations. He was middle-aged and bald. A thin pair of tinted designer glasses was balanced on his nose, and a collection of ornate jewelry hung around his neck.

"Who is he?"

"His name is not important, especially as he changes it every couple of weeks. Just remember that face, that's his current one. He changes that too. He'll be expecting you. When you meet him, hand him this case."

Basilisk beckoned and a technician came over with a slim black briefcase. Basilisk flicked it open and all the boys gasped. The case was filled with bricks of cash.

"The ransom?" asked Jake.

"Most of it. What the blood-sucking drilling technician didn't, ha, *drill* out of me. One point five million exactly." Basilisk shot a glance at Scuffer, whose hand was reaching toward the cash. "Don't get any ideas. Give him the case and he will give you the explosive. Then simply teleport back here."

Scuffer rubbed his sweaty palms against his jeans. An idea occurred to him. "If we're going with Hunter, does that mean we get superpowers too?"

Basilisk barked a laugh. "Powers are for those we deem worthy. You're now his henchmen, so you get to have fun with these." The supervillain walked across to a stack of long plastic military-green trunks with numbers stenciled on the side. He flipped one open, revealing a cache of rifles.

"Guns!" squeaked Knuckles, his voice breaking again.

"Very special guns," Basilisk said, lifting one out. "A little invention of my own. I call them resin-rifles."

The villain aimed the rifle at Big Tony and fired, almost point-blank.

Snow drifted down, obliterating any defining line between the ground and the horizon. Already it was a good eight inches deep around Jake's boots, and he had to stomp to keep warm. None of the guys had been dressed to travel somewhere so cold. Basilisk had given them all gloves, plain black uniforms, and matching long coats that stretched to their knees and concealed the resin-rifles perfectly. But they were not exactly warm.

Big Tony rubbed his ribs. They were still sore from where Basilisk had shot him with the rifle. It had fired a thick gluey blob that had expanded across his chest, seeping around his wide frame and pinning him to the floor like a fly trapped in amber. A demonstration of the potent nonlethal weapon, Basilisk had said.

Then he had taken Jake to a computer terminal so he could select his powers, and instructed Jake on how to use the teleportation ability.

If Jake touched the others, they would be teleported with him. All he had to do was clear his mind and think of the location he wanted to travel to. Not just the name, he had to have a clear concept of where the place was in the world, and an accurate idea of what it looked like. Basilisk had shown him pictures of quiet side roads that ran close to Red Square. It was dangerous to suddenly appear in the middle of the famous plaza, as there were sure to be police, pedestrians, and tourists with cameras.

And now here they were in Russia. Big Tony was having a rough time, and threw up again the moment they appeared in the snowy street. But Scuffer and Knuckles swapped a high five.

"Awesome!" shouted Knuckles.

"That rocks, Hunter!" Scuffer laughed in delight. Jake had to silence them. Luckily they had arrived unseen, and it was a short walk to Red Square.

It was starting to get dark and streetlights had begun to flick on, but the square was still busy with people.

The sheer scale of the place surprised them, stretching almost a thousand feet long and almost two hundred feet wide. It was *vast*. At one end, to the south-east, stood the magnificent multicolored onion domes of Saint Basil's Cathedral. Even bathed in floodlights and masked by driving snow, he had to admit it looked impressive.

The cathedral allowed him to get his bearings. Basilisk's instructions meant that the illuminated, tiered square building close by was Lenin's Mausoleum, the resting place of one of Russia's most famous leaders. Lines of people were waiting to go into the tomb and look upon the embalmed body on display.

On the opposite side of the square a lone figure stood waiting for them. Dressed in a thick black coat, and with the physique of an elephant, the man remained impassive as Jake and his crew strolled over.

Jake's fingers tightened around the case handle. He was carrying an awful lot of money, and people would do silly things for such amounts. Since they had teleported, Scuffer and Knuckles had talked constantly about taking the money and running.

"Typical Scuffer," thought Jake. "Forget the marvels of being transported to a tropical island and then on to Moscow in the blink of an eye." All that drama was lost the moment Scuffer had seen the cash.

They were halfway across the square when Jake

realized his friends had lapsed into silence. Then he felt the hard prod of a rifle barrel in the back of his spine. Scuffer whispered close to his ear. "Sorry, dude. Nothin' personal."

Jake hissed under his breath. "That's a nonlethal weapon, you dope."

"It'll stick you to the spot, superboy, and three of 'em will hurt like hell."

Jake stopped and gave that some silent thought. Scuffer became impatient and pressed the barrel into his back for emphasis. "Just keep walkin' past Frankenstein there, like we're not the ones he's lookin' for."

Jake was forced to change course away from the large man as though they were just another bunch of tourists. Scuffer guided him along the side of the vast building in front, walking northwest toward the floodlit Historical Museum. Pure white snow clung to the side of the museum; a single golden dome poked upward and made the whole thing look like a wedding cake.

"Steady now, and don't try an' use those powers of yours?"

Jake considered teleporting away, but remembered Basilisk telling him that it would take a while for that power to recharge itself before he could use it again. Plus he didn't want to lose face by returning to Basilisk empty-handed.

"I thought we were friends?" Jake said through gritted

teeth. He looked around for an opportunity to escape, but there were too many tourists for him to use his powers.

"Friendship's a weird thing, ain't it? I mean, what kind of friend would hide the fact he had superpowers? A pretty bad one's the answer. You're just not the friend type, are ya?"

Jake felt his temples throb. He couldn't believe a pal was robbing him. Ex-pal, he corrected himself.

Several mean-looking armed policemen stood in front of the museum, joking together and rubbing their hands against the cold. Scuffer looked for a way to avoid them and shoved Jake down a wide street that was lined with cars, but devoid of tourists.

"Now stop. Let go of the case and we'll leave you here with Fat Tony."

"*Big* Tony—and why me? I should have a share!"

"Scuff, turn around and walk away. I'll forget you're trying to rob me," Jake said in a voice that trembled with the hatred he suddenly felt for his former friend.

"Give it to me." Scuffer pulled the case, but Jake held it firmly. "I'm warnin' you, Hunter."

Jake slowly turned around, his vision becoming red-tinged, as if somebody had put a colored filter over his eyes. His perception had changed; the faintest of electrical currents flowing through Scuffer's body were clearly visible, through his clothing and collecting in his brain, which looked like an anthill. Jake didn't have time to wonder what was happening.

Scuffer's mouth hung open at Jake's demonic appearance—his skin was as pale as the snow and his eyes glowed red. Scuffer's arm swung limp, now aiming the rifle at the floor. He became aware of a terrified voice at his shoulder and a corner of his mind realized that it was Knuckles.

"Shoot him! Quick!"

Scuffer's brain started working again and he brought the gun level—just as Jake lashed out.

Concentric silver circles extended from Jake's hand and expanded around Scuffer, freezing him to the spot. It looked as if multiple pulsing hula hoops surrounded him from head to foot. Scuffer screamed; the intensity of the pulsing increased until there was a violent implosion of air—even the falling snow was momentarily sucked toward the spot where Scuffer *used* to be.

Jake was shell-shocked as the red mist faded. He stared at his own hands.

"What've you done to Scuff?" bleated Knuckles, stepping back a pace. "Did you kill him?"

Jake had no idea if he had, but he suddenly recalled that Knuckles had been encouraging Scuffer's betrayal of him. Jake raised his hands menacingly toward him.

"Why don't you find out?" growled Jake.

Knuckles's eyes were as wide as saucers. He threw

his rifle down, turned, slipped on the icy snow, and ran off as fast as he could. Jake exhaled deeply; it would be interesting to find out how Knuckles would manage in Russia with no money or passport and zero knowledge of the language.

Jake became aware that Big Tony was standing at his shoulder, laughing as he watched Knuckles slip and slide as he fled. "Ha-ha! Look at him! Loser!" Jake turned to face him, his eyes turning back to normal. Big Tony's laughter faded and he raised his hands in surrender when he saw Jake's black look. "I didn't know what they were going to do. I swear! They were going to leave me with you, remember? They even called me fat!"

"Let's go, *now*," Jake snarled.

They marched back into Red Square, toward the hulking man who hadn't moved a muscle. Jake barely came up to the man's broad shoulders. He indicated the case.

"I have the money."

The bouncer nodded slightly and walked away. With no indication what to do, Jake and Big Tony followed him toward the cathedral. As they got closer, Jake could see a road alongside the cathedral where a black limousine was waiting, engine running. Their escort rapped on the window, which rolled down with an electric whine. Inside sat the man from Basilisk's photographs. He eyed

A Plan Unveiled

Jake up and down, and when he spoke it was with a heavy Russian accent.

"You types are getting younger each time. You have the money?"

The man took Jake's offered case with hands that had sovereign gold rings on every finger. He flipped the catch open and casually flicked through the neatly stacked bills, before nodding in satisfaction. He looked back at Jake.

"Tell your master it was a pleasure doing business as usual. Your merchandise is in the trunk. Don't worry, I practically own the police force here. Nobody will pay you any attention."

Jake had flinched at the word "master," and decided he needed to clarify things with Basilisk when he returned. Jake gave a curt nod to the man, then walked around to the limo's trunk as it automatically clicked open.

Inside was a black backpack. Jake carefully opened the zipper, and he and Big Tony stared inside for what seemed like an eternity. The bomb was the size and shape of a football, with several spars running from it to keep it from rolling around. There was a single slot in the side where the detonator would presumably plug. It had no display screen for a fancy countdown like he'd seen in films. Only one thing was clear; on the side of the device was a familiar yellow warning triangle, emblazoned with three triangular black lines projecting from a small circle: a radiation symbol.

Jake had just bought a nuclear bomb.

Then a familiar whispering voice from behind sent a feeling of dread through him.

"Hands up, Hunter. Or this time you won't be walking away!"

Reality Strikes

The orange sun balanced on the horizon like an overripe apricot. The desert had a magnifying effect as it dipped over the sand dunes of the United Arab Emirates and far-off Saudi Arabia. Basilisk was not looking at the celestial display but at the towering oil rig that stood in the tranquil waters of the Persian Gulf. A fiery plume flickered continuously from a chimney, burning waste gas and acting as a beacon.

Basilisk flew low over the water. He had to approach the platform with stealth, since armed naval vessels constantly patrolled the water on the lookout for pirates and terrorists. At this stage in the operation he couldn't risk any problems, and that's why he had taken the most potentially dangerous part of the plan himself. If Doc Tempest had betrayed him, then it would be here the Enforcers would pounce. All Hunter had to do was pay the Russian contact and return to the base with the warhead. That was tantamount to walking to the store to buy milk.

Ahead he could make out the helicopter landing pad

poking from the side of the rig. He swooped close to the massive steel legs of the structure, then pulled vertically up, approaching the landing pad directly underneath.

Ruben Carlisse was a tall Dutch scientist and an expert on deep-core drilling. He had planned and led many successful drilling operations for major oil companies around the world, and had a reputation for being able to dig for anything. He had been approached by a mysterious contact who had agreed to pay an obscene amount of money for his services, with the only condition that the nature of the job remained a secret. He had been fine with that: most of Ruben's deals were made under the cloak of secrecy. Drilling for oil and gas deposits was a multi-billion-dollar, cutthroat business.

He paced nervously back and forth next to a closed elevator doorway that led to the main decks of the oil rig. The heat was suffocating, and he only wore a short-sleeved shirt and shorts that ran to his bony knees. He clutched a leather satchel to his chest and searched the sky. He couldn't see any sign of the helicopter that was supposed to pick him up. He lowered his gaze—and was shocked to see Basilisk rise from the side of the rig like an angel of death, arms folded and cape dramatically billowing. The twilight assisted in obscuring Basilisk's features, and Ruben could only see a pair of blazing electric-blue eyes.

Reality Strikes

Ruben's logical mind tried to figure out how the man in front of him appeared to be flying. There was no question of using wires, and human flight was simply not possible. It must be some elaborate illusion. But why go to all that trouble?

"Ruben Carlisse, come with me."

Ruben looked around in confusion. Where was he supposed to go? He was instantly suspicious that this was a ruse.

"First of all, my fee?"

"Paid directly to your Swiss account as instructed. Check if you must, but hurry."

Ruben's eyes never left the figure that drifted impossibly across the landing pad. He reached into his case and pulled out his mobile phone. He dialed one of the preset buttons and was put through to his bank's automated system. He thumbed in his account number and access code, and a synthesized voice confirmed that his bank balance had just substantially increased. He hung up and faced Basilisk with newfound respect.

"So, a legitimate deal then? Thank you. How are we to leave?"

A chorus of solid *click-clacks* got their attention. It was the sound of twenty high-powered Enforcer rifles being chambered. A swarm of red dots appeared all over Basilisk—laser sights from Enforcers who materialized around the landing pad. Five had taken sniper positions in the gantry of the drilling shaft that towered above them.

Ruben's hands shot up and he looked around in terror. "Don't shoot! Don't shoot! I had no idea who he was!"

An amplified voice echoed across the pad. "Basilisk, descend to the platform and put your hands behind your head."

Basilisk was surrounded. He landed on his knees. The Enforcers, dressed head to toe in black body armor, stepped closer, weapons never straying from their target.

"It's over, Basilisk," growled a muscular Chinese man with black sergeant stripes on his sleeve. "Betrayed by your own people. Must be the first time the Council has called us up with some good news. You must have done something real crazy to annoy them. Diablo Island for you. Got a nice comfy cell just waiting for you."

Basilisk lowered his head, facing Ruben, who was looking around like a trapped animal.

"You better hit the deck," whispered Basilisk. Ruben looked questioningly at him. "Do it . . . NOW!"

The terror of the situation had turned Ruben's legs to jelly, so falling flat on his face required no effort at all. The moment he was down Basilisk leaped to his feet.

"I'm not coming with you today, gentlemen. I have a prior engagement." As he had anticipated, the Enforcers hesitated to fire. They had circled him and so risked shooting their colleagues opposite.

"Shoot him!" bellowed the sergeant as Basilisk spread his arms.

Gunfire erupted from the snipers first. The bullets passed right through the supervillain as if he were a phantom, and pinged from the landing pad. The Enforcers around him carefully took aim and fired. Again the shots passed harmlessly through—one soldier's bullet clipped his opposite companion's arm, drawing blood.

A blinding glow shone from within Basilisk; his skin cracked as if he were made of plaster. The troops shielded their eyes; Ruben covered his head with both arms . . .

. . . as Basilisk exploded.

Flechettes went in every direction, hitting every Enforcer around him. The darts gouged into some of the soldiers' legs, dropping them to the deck in agony before the poisoned tips took effect. Others staggered off the edge and fell the hundred feet into the Gulf. The darts even hit the snipers perched on the gantry, and they fell, thudding hard onto the deck.

It was over in seconds.

Ruben peeked from behind his arms. Everybody around him was down. He heard a couple of groans, but he was sure most were dead.

The real Basilisk soared from where he had been hiding under the pad and landed on the deck with a

thump. He picked up a small circular device that was lying in front of Ruben. He pressed a button and a ghostly three-dimensional image of himself flickered, then died.

"Holographic decoy," Basilisk said with a hint of pride. "Not bad at all." He had hidden beneath the pad and let the decoy take his place as a contingency in case he had been betrayed. It had been a smart move. He would deal with Tempest in due time, but right now he had bigger plans.

Ruben's voice quivered. "You . . . you killed them?"

"Poison-tipped darts. I was going to arm it with explosives but this whole oil rig would have been blown sky-high. That would have attracted too much attention." Ruben felt a strong grip around his wrist and was pulled to his feet. "You've been paid for your services. They start now. We're leaving."

Ruben was still confused. He looked around for an approaching helicopter. "How?"

"We teleport out. This is going to feel very unpleasant," Basilisk said with a trace of mirth.

Jake's entire body tensed and he slowly turned around. Big Tony already had his hands in the air and was shaking from both the cold and fear. A young man in his early twenties, with a pale face and jet-black hair, was regarding them impassively. While he looked unfamiliar, there was no mistaking the voice of Chameleon.

"Couldn't you have picked a face that was less ugly?" said Jake, his voice sounding harder than he felt.

"Quite the wit, Hunter. And to think your mother actually finds you charming."

"My mother? You better not have—"

"You're hardly in the position to be threatening me. I paid a visit to your family. Oh, don't worry, they are very well. In fact, better than ever now that they don't have a thoughtless, arrogant son to worry about."

Jake bit his tongue. Dragging the parents into an argument was an old schoolyard psychological game that always got kids angry. He knew better than to believe a single word. "How have you been following me?"

"Between you, the Council of Evil, and this nuke, I've been quite busy. Shame I don't get air miles. I've been on the trail of this stolen warhead for some time, and the moment an informer had told us that Basilisk was planning a big explosion . . . well, I knew where he'd be buying the bomb for *that*. So I came straight here—after I'd got out of the pool of blood and glass you left me in back at your school. You're not the only one who can teleport, you know."

The large Russian minder who was waiting patiently

at the front of the limo turned and irritably snapped at Jake.

"Hurry up. Take your package."

Jake frowned. "He can't see you?"

"Or hear me. Another of my *many* skills. I'm afraid that the game is up. I'm taking you in."

"What? Into supervillain prison?" Jake scoffed.

"You haven't heard of Diablo Island Penitentiary?" Jake must have looked startled because Chameleon smiled like a predator. "It appears you haven't! Perhaps Basilisk neglected to mention that, like he evidently failed to tell you *lots* of other important facts. Well then, you are in for a treat. They don't have lenient sentences for the likes of you."

"He forced me to come along!" blubbered Big Tony.

Prison was a new concept for Jake. He had never really considered the consequences of his actions. Although he'd been in trouble before he'd never actually seen prison as an outcome, especially now that he was a supervillain. Even when he found himself embroiled in the kidnapping, the thought of what might happen to him if he was caught never really crossed his mind. He had been more worried about what Basilisk might say than anything else.

With superpowers at his disposal, he knew for sure that there was no way he was going to spend any time in a cell. He didn't hesitate. He snatched the backpack from the trunk and took off—flying toward the storm clouds at such a speed that there wasn't even time to register Chameleon's expression.

At this pace the snow felt like stones striking his face, but the weight of the backpack was slowing Jake down. The dense nuclear material was far heavier than the dead weight of the Ukrainian had been when he'd had to lug him onto the roof.

He briefly thought about the wrongness of leaving Big Tony behind, but then again his "friend" had been quick to abandon him in a moment of fear. Jake was feeling callous enough to forget all about him. In fact, the speed with which his only three friends had turned on him from the lure of money or the threat of danger had surprised him.

Worse still, that left the unscrupulous villain Basilisk as the only person who hadn't betrayed him. He had done nothing more harmful than lie.

A plume of fire shot past Jake. He spiraled around to loop both arms through the pack's straps and risked a glance down. It was a giddying experience as the ground rotated; he could see Big Tony staring up at him. Chameleon was already flying in pursuit and had covered half the distance toward him. The superhero discharged another tongue of flame from his leading hand, but that went wide.

The higher Jake climbed the slower he moved with the

added weight. That meant racing Chameleon into the clouds was not an option. Instead Jake banked sharply back toward the ground, aiming for the Moskva River. The maneuver threw off his pursuer, who then followed in a yawning curve that helped increase Jake's lead.

Jake swept low over the river, and was thankful for the veil of snow and twilight that hung over the water. He hoped no one on the river could see him—he didn't need yet another police chase on top of everything else. He increased his speed with the simple act of stretching forward. Now he was moving so fast that, as he took the bend in the river, it felt more like one of his car-racing games on his console. A glance behind revealed that Chameleon was slowly gaining. They were both so low to the water that their displaced air pressure formed wakes across its surface, like passing speedboats.

Jake weaved around ships and shot under a bridge. He had the odd sensation that his teleportation powers were almost recharged. He just needed to last a few more seconds. He navigated through a tight S-bend. As he pulled out of the sharp curve, a large cargo container ship filled his view. Jake tensed and threw himself violently sideways—but only succeeded in corkscrewing himself through the air. He narrowly missed the hull of the boat, and was so close that his belt buckle raked the side of the ship and kicked up a spray of sparks. Jake could feel the friction heat against his belly.

Reality Strikes

He'd lost his tail, but he knew it was only a matter of time before Chameleon reappeared. He wished he'd downloaded some aquatic powers to avoid this chase.

The river turned sharply again to his left and swept under another bridge. As he tried to ready himself to teleport, envisioning Basilisk's subterranean hangar, he felt a sudden weight tug his leg, and his airspeed dropped. He looked round to see Chameleon clutching his boot and grinning at him.

"Not so fast, Hunter! If you go, I go!"

How did Chameleon know he was going to teleport? Was he telepathic? Jake knew he couldn't teleport with the hero touching him, as that would lead him right back to their secret headquarters.

"Give yourself up, Hunter," said Chameleon. "I'm not letting go!"

Jake brought the heel of his other foot down on his enemy's fingers, but it was like hitting rubber. Chameleon didn't betray a single flicker of pain.

Another bridge loomed, heavy with traffic, and Jake had an idea. He changed direction. Chameleon tried to get a better grip on Jake with his other hand. The hero was so intent on staying attached to Jake that he didn't notice they had abruptly ascended.

Jake roared *over* the bridge with Chameleon hanging on behind—and narrowly missing being splattered against the parapet. Chameleon's grunt of relief quickly

turned to astonishment when he realized Jake was flying low over the heavy traffic on the bridge itself. Chameleon heard the deep honk of a truck horn and turned in time to see an eighteen-wheeler fill his world.

Jake felt Chameleon release his grip and at the same instant he heard a colossal smash of a windshield shattering. Chameleon hit the truck like a bug. Jake could see no sign of the hero, only a shower of glass peppering the vehicles on either side. The truck slammed on its brakes in a hiss of compressed air and a screech of burning rubber. Pedestrians on the bridge watched as the truck broadsided half a dozen cars and the rear trailer threatened to jackknife.

Fortunately, people were so riveted to the crash they didn't look up. Nobody noticed Jake powering directly toward the clouds. The clamor of traffic and car horns drowned out the faintest thunderclap as Jake Hunter teleported away, without his friends, but with a nuclear warhead.

The hangar was dimly lit when Jake appeared. He wobbled on shaky legs and gingerly placed the backpack on a workbench so that he wouldn't drop it. He had been pretty sure that the bomb wouldn't detonate from a simple knock, but was uncertain how it would respond after being teleported about seven thousand miles.

Reality Strikes

After waiting for the wave of dizziness to pass, Jake headed for the passage that led to the command center. He was feeling weary and irritable as he recalled Chameleon's words. The superjerk had spoken to his parents, and Jake couldn't shake the ominous feeling that Chameleon had done something bad to them.

As he got closer to the command center, he became aware that the usual operation background noise was no longer there. However, he could just hear the faint sound of Basilisk's voice.

Curious, Jake edged forward to the end of the passage and froze as the door automatically spiraled open. Basilisk was standing with his back to him, and apparently hadn't heard the door open. The screen had eight separate images across it, each with a different person peering out. Jake was at an angle to the screen, so the dark contrast washed out their features; nonetheless he could still make out a range of bizarrely shaped heads. It was clear that whoever was on-screen was displeased with Basilisk, who was nervously shifting his weight from one leg to the other. Jake tiptoed into the room and hid under the nearest desk.

"The Council warned it was ill advised, Basilisk," boomed the somber voice of one of the figures.

"Not that your opinion matters anymore. And I disagree. Hunter has exceeded your predictions."

Jake perked up the moment his name was mentioned.

Who were these people and why were they talking about him?

"You have had no approval to recruit! And especially not him! That is a direct violation of Council rules, yet you still continue to indoctrinate the boy!"

"I am no longer a member of the Council! I left because of your stupid rules!"

"We threw you out! We'd gathered enough information about your activities to warrant our intervention."

Basilisk sneered. "Ah, yes. You sent the weather boy to do your work. Well, it failed—and I will deal with Tempest when I deal with the rest of you."

"An idle threat! And Tempest has served us well. Even as we speak he is rendezvousing to be brought back into the folds of the Council. You are on your own!"

"I could wipe you both out together. Save some time."

A chorus of squeals erupted from the wall panel. Jake heard the words "insolence!" and "traitor!" Basilisk chuckled, amused at the reaction.

"Not that we'd meet him in person," snarled the main voice again.

"You are all cowards to the last. And you wonder why I've broken away."

"We *threw you out*," reminded a female voice.

"No, I left before you could."

Jake frowned. He remembered Basilisk telling him

that the Council was a governing body, designed to keep villains in check. But Basilisk was no longer a part of this? Was he an outlaw? Jake tried to get his head around the concept of a criminal who had broken the criminals' own laws. Jake's old black-and-white view of the world would have branded Basilisk as either a good guy or the worst criminal of the bunch. But after the last week he was fast learning that such polar opinions meant nothing. The truth was always something more complicated.

Jake didn't consider himself an *evil* person, but then again he had just bought a nuclear bomb from, he assumed, the Russian Mafia. Suddenly, accidentally burning down the classroom seemed a petty crime.

"Your rules are antiquated!" Basilisk shook his fist at the screen. "You have no idea of the boy's potential! There is more to him than what a simple online diagnostic test can show."

There was a moment's silence as the figures on-screen muttered among themselves. The only phrases Jake caught were "anomaly," "genetic matching," and "database corruption," all of which made zero sense to him. The woman's voice rose again.

"Until we have further chance to investigate this situation, you must not use him as an asset and you have to turn yourself over to us."

"No," bellowed Basilisk. "Plans are in motion that even you cannot stop!"

"Your scheme is extreme, Basilisk," came a new gurgling voice. "Your calculations are in error and you pose an unacceptable threat to the world. You risk wiping out life as we know it and therefore your own allies!"

Jake could now see that Basilisk's fists were balled, and his shoulders squared in anger. "You are no allies of mine! The Council is archaic and grows weak!"

Jake reasoned that if Basilisk's plan was really crazy enough to wipe out all life on earth it was in essence a suicide mission—meaning Basilisk and Jake would die too.

And my family . . . and Lorna, added a small voice at the back of his mind, a conscience he had not heard for a long time. He resolved that he would go home and see his parents and sister as soon as he had talked to Basilisk.

Basilisk's voice raised in fury. "A new generation is rising that will see you extinct! And I will lead that revolution!" He stabbed a button on the control panel and all the screens went dead.

Jake pressed himself farther under the desk and hoped that he hadn't been spotted eavesdropping. Basilisk spun on his heels and stalked into his side office. Only when the door had closed did Jake expel a long sigh.

He was out of his league in trouble, and he knew the *right thing* to do would be to turn Basilisk in to the authorities. But when had Jake Hunter ever really done the right thing? Besides, he was now implicated in the madness. There was no way he could talk himself out of this situation.

He climbed out from underneath the desk and sat in a swivel chair. His eyes felt heavy, so he closed them, propping his head up with his arms as he worked through the new events.

Basilisk was working directly against the Council, and had said they would soon be "extinct." And now Jake remembered bucket-headed Doc Tempest saying it was a good thing Basilisk had "broken away." Jake had heard the term "loose cannon" before and it seemed appropriate here.

For some reason the Council knew about Jake and were against him. In fairness, Basilisk had defended him. His head pounded from a growing headache as he tried to rationalize.

His so-called friends hadn't attempted to defend him; in fact all three had taken the first available opportunity to turn on him. Did that make Basilisk his friend? In his experience, friends lied to each other all the time, but still remained friends. And while Basilisk's plan was absurd, Jake didn't think for a moment it could be *that* dangerous. Basilisk wasn't the suicidal type and he clearly had plans for the future, for leading the next generation. If it only took one explosion to rock the world, then the earth would have been destroyed many years ago.

It had to be a bluff. His eyes flicked back open. The new thoughts made sense. Basilisk had originally told him that he was keeping the plan quiet for security reasons—no doubt that meant from traitors like Tempest. Basilisk wouldn't initiate a plan to kill himself, so the obvious conclusion was that detonating the bomb was a bluff, and his real scheme was some kind of attack against this sinister Council of Evil.

Jake could feel his superpowers ebbing. He now recognized the symptoms, which left him very tired and weak. He felt a strong desire to download more and wondered if this was what addiction felt like.

With a gentle swish, the door opened and the technicians entered carrying food and Styrofoam coffee cups. Obviously somewhere deeper in the complex was a dining hall. Jake's stomach rumbled with the glorious prospect of food. He gave his chair to one of the technicians, an old guy in his fifties, who reminded Jake of his own grandfather. The man nodded politely, and Jake thought, a little respectfully too.

That was one thing Jake could get used to: being respected rather than shouted at and ordered around. Basilisk reappeared from his side office.

"Hunter! Have you just arrived?"

"Yes," lied Jake.

"And the bomb?"

"You could have told me it was a nuclear warhead,"

said Jake. He tried to sound angry, but was just too zonked.

"That would have been an extra concern you did not need. Where is it?"

"In the hangar."

"And you had no trouble?"

Jake laughed at the irony. "Do you mean apart from my three friends turning against me and another run-in with that shape-shifting freak?"

"Chameleon? He found you so quickly?" Basilisk looked away, presumably staring thoughtfully into space. His cowl never lifted, and Jake felt curious, for the first time, as to what Basilisk actually looked like. Why was he concealing his face? That was another mystery, but his stomach reminded him there were more pressing matters at hand.

"I'm going to get something to eat now. Then I want to go home and see if my parents are okay. *After that* you can fill me in on the next part of this scheme of yours. And will we get to keep the money this time?"

"If this works, we get to keep *everything*," purred Basilisk. "But your parents—"

Jake had been ready for an argument. "You picked me, remember? So if you want us to work *together*, then I'm going to see them. Just for a few minutes to make sure the Enforcers haven't got to them. No arguments." He stared levelly at Basilisk. Or at least where he thought Basilisk's eyes should be.

"Very well. But before we go I have one last important task for you."

Jake sighed; Basilisk was pushing him around again. "Can't it wait?" he snapped.

"No. It's to show you how much I trust you, and how important you are to the success of this operation. I want you to be the one who announces our intentions to the world!"

Revelations

Mud sucked around Jake's boots as they teleported into the field close to his house. Jake eagerly started forward, but Basilisk cautioned him.

"Be careful. If the Enforcers have been here, they will have set perimeter motion alarms."

Jake didn't respond. He was feeling exhausted and there were so many unanswered questions about Basilisk that he no longer knew who to trust. He pushed forward through the trees on his own.

One phrase from a video game ran through Jake's mind: "the point of no return." It meant that you had traveled too far to turn back, since the destination was closer. And that's exactly how Jake had felt when, before they left the island, Basilisk had placed him in front of a camera.

Jake had read from a preprepared sheet hanging just to the side of the camera. They had to record the demand twice because his mouth dried up. Basilisk had assured him that his face would be obscured and his voice digitally altered to hide his true identity.

Jake wondered why Basilisk had not announced his intentions to the world himself, but the question remained unspoken, as he didn't want to provoke Basilisk and ruin his chances of seeing his parents. And that was another point that irked Jake. If he was free, then why did he have to ask permission?

The patch of woodland gave way to Jake's yard and he could see the house ahead. Warm lights blazed from within, which was an encouraging sign. Jake was slowly advancing across the lawn when something caught his attention—a small orb poking from the grass next to a garden gnome. That was new.

Jake carefully approached it, and a small whirling noise inside made him freeze. It sounded like a tiny camera moving. It was one of the motion sensors that Basilisk had warned him about. He had said they were configured to detect the altered DNA that supers possess, so they wouldn't go off every time a bird moved past.

He cursed his clumsiness. The Enforcers now knew where he was. He didn't have much time.

He tried the back door but it was locked. He was sure that only his family was home, but still he proceeded cautiously. He climbed onto the porch, inched open his bedroom window, and dropped inside. It took a few moments for his eyes to adjust to the darkness, and when they did he felt a chill run through his body.

The room was empty.

Revelations

All his possessions were gone. His posters, his computer, Xbox, and even the mirror that was covered in stickers and postcards were gone. The room smelled strongly of fresh paint. It was as though somebody had tried to erase any trace of him.

Downstairs he heard strains of music and laughter from the television. He crept out onto the landing and poked his head into his sister's room. That was as messy as usual.

The floorboards creaked under his weight as he stealthily walked downstairs. In the living room his parents were watching TV and enjoying a glass of wine. Beth sat with her feet up on an armchair, reading a book. His father's deep laugh reassured him that everything was okay.

"Hi," he said nervously.

Nobody stirred. They must be really annoyed to ignore him like this. He stepped into the room.

"I'm back!"

Still no response. Now Jake was hurt. He purposefully stood between his parents and the television.

"Hello? I'm back. Your son has returned!"

His father just belly laughed again at an inane joke from the TV sitcom. Jake frowned; nothing felt right. He waved his hands in front of their faces, and noticed his parents' expressions turn glassy, as though trying to focus behind him. Beth looked up.

"When is that pizza going to come? I'm starving."

"Shouldn't be too long," their mother replied.

"What's going on?" Jake demanded. "I'm not invisible. I know you can see me. Hello!"

Their ignorance was so frustrating that Jake swiped a picture off the mantel in exasperation. It smashed on the floor but nobody took the slightest notice. Jake was about to shout when he noticed the photograph. It had been taken on a family holiday about five years earlier. It was one of the few family photographs they were all in.

Except now Jake was missing.

He gaped at the picture. Somebody had removed him completely. He knew a good computer art program could do that, but seeing the effect firsthand was chilling. Jake felt numb and his throat was suddenly dry. He gave his family one last look before he ran into the kitchen to gulp down a glass of water. The doorbell rang and he heard Beth leap from her seat.

"Pizza!"

Jake wiped away the sweat that had suddenly formed on his forehead. Chameleon must be responsible for this. Him, the Enforcers, whoever—they were all the same. The so-called goodies were now the bad guys in Jake's book. He glanced around the kitchen and was surprised to see a half-finished meal on the table. Steam drifted from the plates indicating that it was still warm.

Revelations

Jake frowned. Why had they ordered pizza?

The heavy boots from the hallway told him everything he needed to know. The Enforcers had arrived. It must be more mind control. Jake was sure that his family would be as blind to the heavily armed soldiers as they were to him.

Jake ran for the back door; the key was usually in the lock but his fingers grasped empty air. He glanced behind to see two Enforcers push an oblivious Beth against the wall and sprint toward him, rifles gripped with both hands. Luckily the hall was too narrow to allow their bulky frames to wield the weapons.

Basilisk had told Jake that his body couldn't handle any more powers so soon after the last batch, so at that moment he was completely defenseless. Jake didn't hesitate—he grabbed a kitchen chair and smashed it through the glass panels on the back door, then vaulted through the splintered wooden door frame.

He hit the grass and rolled in shards of broken glass, which cut deep into his legs and arms. No sooner had he pulled himself to his feet than the back door blew apart under heavy gunfire, the high-caliber rounds shredding what was left of the solid wood. .

Jake was halfway across the yard by the time an Enforcer had booted his way out and fired into the darkness. Jake heard the shots whiz through the air close by. He must have cut himself badly, as he was

beginning to feel light-headed—then he fell as his legs suddenly gave under him.

He was unconscious before he hit the muddy lawn.

Television stations around the globe received the transmission almost simultaneously. They all had strict instructions on what to do in the event of receiving terrorist demands. The channel controllers contacted their governments, ensuring the broadcast did not leak out and startle the general population.

Forty minutes after the broadcast had been received, world leaders had been plucked from their duties—the German chancellor from an economic press conference; the Australian prime minister from a tour of a local school; the British prime minister from a rowdy session in the House of Commons; and the president of the United States from the golf course. With their assembled chiefs of staff, they watched the transmission. The voice had been digitally dropped an octave and the face was pixilated into tiny blocks that constantly shifted like a swarm of choreographed bees, to form different faces.

"People of the world, I carry a demand that must be met within twenty-four hours. By now your Secret Service departments will be aware of the Core Probe stolen from the Indian Institute of Advanced Technology. A machine that was designed to penetrate down to the earth's core. The Probe is now armed with a ten-megaton nuclear warhead, which will be detonated at the center of the earth."

Across the world, behind closed doors, an outcry went up at these words. The figure continued.

"Should this explode, it will shift the earth off its axis, causing wild tidal shifts and irreversible weather patterns that will radically change the world's environment, and destroy your rich economies. You have the power to prevent this. This transmission includes digitally encoded bank details for depositing two billion dollars."

Again, more muttering around the globe, all commenting on the typical greed-driven extortion plied by these villains. But the message continued, surprising them all.

"In addition, we demand military assets from various countries. From the United States, their entire fleet of B2 Stealth Bombers. From the United Kingdom, their entire Naval Fleet. From the European Union their fleets of Typhoon Fighters. From . . ."

The list was extensive and caused a mass furor among the world's leaders. Within minutes, they were on the phones to one another in blind panic. This maniac wasn't simply demanding money; he was piecing together his own massive army, using the best technology the world had to offer—in effect disarming nations and leaving them open to attack by the new rogue army.

Scientists ran figures and soon opinions became divided. Some thought a single nuclear detonation at the earth's core wouldn't do anything, and the warhead would probably melt before it reached its target. Others pointed out that it was an unexplored area of science and there was a danger that any detonation could have an adverse effect on the earth's orbit; a simple demonstration was presented over a video link to world leaders. A spinning gyroscope remained perfectly balanced on a table, but it only took a gentle finger poke, representing a nuclear blast under the earth's mantle, to send it skittering to the floor.

Jake flicked his eyes open, and instantly wished he hadn't. The room's lights appeared to burn intensely, giving him a headache. He was lying down on a hard surface. He squinted and used his hand to shield his eyes.

"Easy" said an unfamiliar voice. Jake slowly opened his eyes. The friendly face of a plump woman was looking at him with concern. "'Feeling better?"

"Uh, yeah." Feeling groggy, he pulled himself up. He noticed the ceiling light was made up of several high-intensity bulbs arrayed in a circle, like he'd seen in an operating room when he'd had his appendix removed as a child. Medical equipment was packed into this

Revelations

room. His fears that the Enforcers had captured him vanished when he noticed the rough carved walls that indicated he was back in Basilisk's subterranean lair.

The villain himself was standing across the room, staring at Jake with his smoldering neon gaze. "Is the boy all right now?"

Jake realized he was wearing just his boxer shorts. He flexed his fingers, noticing that they were unusually pale. But, despite the headache, he was feeling stronger. He noticed a bloodstained metal dish that had been placed on the side. It had several jagged pieces of glass in it. Scabs on his arms and legs had already begun to fade. A cable ran into his arm, linked to a computer.

"He'll be fine," the doctor said as she studied a computer screen. "Remarkable though. I have never seen a reaction like this before."

Jake cocked his head. "A reaction to what?"

Before the doctor could open her mouth, Basilisk took a step forward, and dismissed her with a gesture. "That will be all, doctor. Leave us."

The doctor nodded to Jake and spun on her heels, quickly leaving the chamber. Basilisk began pacing the room.

"Your demand to the world has been delivered, anonymously of course. Our technicians ensured your face was unrecognizable."

"Great," Jake said without enthusiasm. He had too

many questions that required answers. "What happened?"

"Chameleon and the Enforcers got to your parents. They suspected you would return, although evidently not so soon or they would have been better prepared. I reached you when you passed out, and we teleported back here."

"My family . . . they didn't recognize me at all."

"There are mind-control powers out there that can be more devastating than an energy bolt or a death ray. Chameleon used another hero to telepathically erase you from your family's mind. So much so that their brains refused to see you or acknowledge your existence. It effectively rendered you invisible to them. I saw what happened in there. All they had to do was incinerate your possessions and digitally remove you from photographs."

Jake stared at the wall as he put his clothes back on.

"When your sister answered the door, she truly did think it was a pizza delivery. Ours is a world your family will no longer see."

The memory of his parents' vacant expressions made him feel sick. He had ceased to exist to them. A morbid thought crept into his mind—if they had died, he would never be able to see them again. But this felt *worse*. He could see them . . . but they had no idea he had ever existed.

Revelations

It was as if *he* were a ghost. In effect he was now an orphan.

He fought back tears. "Is it reversible?"

"I do not know. There could be terrible repercussions to reversing a memory block. I have heard of people going crazy from such attempts, falling into vegetative states. And to be truly effective, you need the Prime who took the powers to restore them."

Jake silently vowed revenge. Then what the doctor had said about "reaction" snagged his thoughts. He looked at Basilisk. "I'm having a bad reaction to the superpowers, aren't I?"

Basilisk stopped pacing, and turned his dark cowl on Jake. "I wouldn't use the term 'bad.' It's most unusual though."

"Will I be okay?"

"You'll live," said Basilisk flatly. "Hunter, there is much happening you don't know."

"And I'm tired of that!" snapped Jake as he stood up. It was only then he noticed the computer he was plugged into was logged on to Villain.net. He yanked the cable from his arm. "So why don't you tell me what this is all about? I've lost my family because of you!"

"It was not I who attacked them, Jake."

Jake wasn't listening; he was too furious to notice it was the first time Basilisk had used his proper name. "You *made* me do that demand! Why didn't you do it yourself? And what's with all the military equipment? I thought the goal here was wealth?"

"The goal is *power*. Wealth is the necessary companion to that. And the armies . . . well, something to negotiate with."

Jake looked back at the Villain.net screen and frowned as he recalled the conversation he'd overheard between Basilisk and the Council. He pointed at the Web site. "You're not supposed to be using this, are you? The Council has banned you."

It was Basilisk's body language that showed his surprise. "How did you know that?"

"I overheard," Jake growled back. For once Basilisk did not intimidate him. He was starting to grasp just how much the villain had been using him. To Jake's surprise Basilisk broke into a deep laugh.

"You truly have a devious mind, Hunter. Spying on me? Excellent. I think it is time you learned about Villain.net and your role in all this." Basilisk theatrically waved his hand around the room.

"My role? You've used me. This is all a bluff, isn't it, so that you can get back at the Council?"

"You are very special, Jake. You are linked to all this in ways you do not yet understand."

Jake leveled his gaze at Basilisk. It made him livid that Basilisk was still being evasive.

Jake felt a rush of power ripple through him and it

dawned on him that he *had* powers. They must have downloaded them into him while he was unconscious. Maybe that's why he felt better? If Basilisk didn't start giving him some straight answers, then he would beat them out of him.

"You'd better start telling me," he said with menace.

"Mr. President?"

The president of the United States looked up from wiping doughnut crumbs from the intelligence report in his hand. His secretary had just entered the Oval Office, wringing her hands nervously. The president licked his fingers clean, then took off his glasses and rubbed his sore eyes. It was late night, or was it early morning? All he knew was that the White House grounds beyond the window were cloaked in darkness.

"Yes?" he said, hoping she was about to offer another pot of coffee. He needed something to keep him going.

"I have an encrypted call from the Enforcers."

The president sighed. When he took office there had been a childlike side to him that had been looking forward to reading about state secrets the public would never be aware of. He had hoped he would finally discover if the government was keeping hidden files on aliens and a flying saucer in storage somewhere. What he hadn't expected was that a whole branch of the government was dedicated to working with, and hiding the existence of, superheroes and villains. The global community had decided that the general public didn't need to know such things, so they worked closely with law enforcement agencies across the world to cover up superactivities and disguise them as terrorist threats or the work of common criminals. That made it difficult for any government to work directly against the super-villain threat. That's where the Enforcers came in.

Originally formed by the United Nations, the Enforcers were essentially a secret army, elite soldiers from around the world who ensured supervillains, and some overzealous superheroes, were kept under control. Since the Enforcers were not allowed to have any superpowers themselves, they relied on the very latest technology and assistance from governments, and on superheroes out in the field who were combating crime on a daily basis.

The president didn't like dealing with the Enforcers, partly because they were not under his direct control, and partly because he thought they had too much power. He had been secretly lobbying for greater restrictions on them. He reached for the phone, and gave his secretary a meaningful look.

"I think more coffee would be in order." His secretary smiled nervously and left quickly. He lifted the receiver to his ear and sat back in his plush leather chair.

Revelations

"This is the president."

"Mister President," said a voice from across the line. It had a gentle Scottish lilt that the President found pleasant to listen to. "We have gathered reliable intelligence on the mastermind behind the new demand and his location. I'm transmitting data to you now."

The president reached across and booted up a computer on the corner of his desk. He typed in a sixteen-digit password, and moments later he accessed a program that decrypted the incoming transmission. It showed a silent video clip of the terrorist's demands.

"Both the picture and audio were digitally altered," continued the voice. "But by a complex process of reversing the algorithms used, we have this."

The pixelated image shifted; millions of tiny pixels moved into the correct position like a rapidly assembling jigsaw. Within seconds the face of a young boy with pale features and spiky blond hair stared out at them. The president inhaled a deep breath.

"It's only a kid! This can't be right!"

"We assure you it is. Since the attack in India we have been tracking this new threat. Chameleon found him."

A school photo of the boy appeared, along with his education record, which the president noticed was poor, and his name: Jake Hunter.

"He's a known troublemaker," the voice continued. "Although nothing on this scale, of course."

The president glanced at a family photo perched on the edge of his desk; he focused on the face of his daughter and a smile flickered across his lips. It was thanks to Chameleon that she was alive, so if that superhero had gathered this intelligence, then he knew it was reliable.

"But this scheme is beyond the skills of a kid, surely?" asked the president.

The voice now sounded reproachful. "No, sir. That would be underestimating the enemy. And Enforcers don't do that. Chameleon has had several skirmishes with our target, and he's had the opportunity to collect DNA samples to authenticate identification."

The president frowned; he was starting to get a little uncomfortable without his team of advisers. "And what did that prove?"

"It proved that Jake Hunter is not who he appears to be. It seems he is a much older villain we've tackled in the past. He's a Prime. You may be familiar with the name Basilisk?"

A chill ran down the president's spine at the very mention of that name and the memory of Basilisk kidnapping his daughter during his first term in office. During the incident he had come face-to-face with Basilisk. And he had seen the menace was an adult. Not this boy.

"Are you saying that this boy *is* Basilisk? That's impossible," he sputtered through dry lips.

"The DNA match is exact. Jake Hunter *is* Basilisk.

The intriguing thing is that they have been seen to-gether. So we're thinking the child may be a clone."

"A clone? Is that possible?"

"That's the only theory that fits right now, since they both share the same DNA. Even twins have separate DNA codes. Chameleon thinks that this boy is display-ing powers beyond what ordinary superheroes are supposed to possess."

The president was out of his league. "I don't under-stand."

"The Hero Foundation wants to bring him in for research. They think he could be a valuable asset. And from our limited intelligence, it seems that the Council of Evil thinks so too. Basilisk has broken away from the Council and is acting independently."

"Good God, that's all we need!"

"We have a positive ID on their location. An air approach is not an option, so to launch an assault we need to request equipment from your Navy Seals, the Sea Crawlers. The navy is giving us static so we need your authorization to get them."

The president peered at the kid's innocent-looking face on the screen, and nodded his approval before real-izing he was still on the telephone.

"Of course, yes. Do whatever it takes to stop this threat. I want him and Basilisk wiped off the face of the planet once and for all!"

* * *

Basilisk paced the room, a habit that Jake now recognized as a nervous one.

"I have told you about Primes. They are people gifted with a range of superpowers from birth. Nowadays they tend to have only three or four abilities at the most, although there are occasional Primes with many more, like there were just decades ago. A private foundation was created to research these powers. They discovered a system that allowed them to band together the incredible gifts and deliver them to people with no powers whatsoever."

"People like me?" said Jake. "So they formed Villain.net?"

"Not initially. The Primes who developed the Web site did not think as grandly as you and me. They were the heroes, intent on spreading their gift to young people in order to develop a new generation of heroes. They created a Web site called Hero.com."

"Hero.com? That name's almost as bad as ours!"

"The name came from the foundation's acronym: the Higher Energy Research Organization. We couldn't think of anything more original for our site, so Villain it was. Like I've said before, these heroes are nothing of the sort. Their Web site serves to spread their propaganda—and they don't seem to mind making a profit from it either!"

Revelations

Jake could see Basilisk was getting angry, and drifting from the subject.

"They charge to download the powers—and they call *us* the crooks! At least with us you get them free." Basilisk shook his head in disbelief. "But they do have a good system; it weeds out the competent from the incompetent, the heroes from the villains. Needless to say, this left the bad guys lagging behind. So the leading villains of the age grouped together to form the Council of Evil. I was once part of that."

"And you stole Hero.com?"

"Why go through the effort and hardship of creating something new when it's much easier to steal one and put your own name on it? The problem lies in the fact that we do not know the limitations of our own site, since we didn't create it. We really just put a new interface on the front, stole a research lab that stored their powers, and added our own."

"And where is all that now?"

"Villain.net is with the Council in their, ha, *secret* location. While the Primes pooled their existing powers, the Council experimented and discovered methods of creating *new* powers, harnessing the very core of what makes any superpower possible."

Jake frowned as the potential of controlling all the possible superpowers struck him. "So you mean you discovered how to grow your own powers?"

"An interesting phrase, but yes, in the same way you can breed dogs that are smaller or have longer ears or shorter tails. Powers can be cultivated."

Silence filled the room. It was so deep that Jake could hear the blood pounding in his ears and the gentle throb of the air-conditioning. He thought about the implications of what he had just learned. If you could develop your own powers then surely there would be no limit to what you could do. You could become . . . a god.

"Combine our unstable home-brewed powers with the fact that we have a site that we don't truly understand the workings of, and you have the potential for side effects. Like the reactions you are experiencing."

"What's wrong with me?"

Basilisk paused, and Jake was beginning to wonder if he had been editing the story, leaving out key bits of information.

"The powers from Villain.net are more potent than its heroic rival," Basilisk continued. "They had to be, because we needed an edge over those irritating do-gooders. So we offered more powers at a stronger dosage, with a downside: they didn't last quite as long. Early test subjects who displayed side effects usually blew apart after a couple of hours."

"They blew up?" cried Jake. "Is that going to happen to me?"

"No, no. At least, I don't think so. That was merely a

teething problem with the Web site." "Some teething problem," thought Jake. "We don't have time to study the site properly, not since we have a constant battle between the sites for dominance. If only we could figure a way of crushing Hero.com."

An idea occurred to Jake, thankfully guiding his over-active imagination away from the fact that he might self-destruct. "Why not create a virus to bring the site down?"

Basilisk stopped pacing and turned to face Jake. His eyes flared bright blue, and excitement made his voice tremble. "What did you say?"

"A computer virus. I used one in school to crash the school computer network."

Basilisk placed a hand on Jake's shoulder in a sign of admiration. "Hunter, that is a genius idea. All this time the Council has been using brute force and stealth tactics to topple the Foundation. And all the time there were villains out there with the necessary skills like Trojan and the dreaded Viral. What a team they would make!" Basilisk's voice sounded dreamy and he seemed lost in a world of plotting.

"Anyway, what has all that got to do with me? Why am I having a reaction?"

"It appears you are becoming addicted to the powers. Your body is thriving on the energy you have with each successful download. And when that power fades your body craves more. In fact, it starts to slowly shut itself down until you download more powers. You have been unconscious for two hours, and during that time our doctor has had to slowly feed a variety of powers from Villain.net into you, just to keep you stable."

"So, if I don't keep downloading powers . . . I'll die?"

"We don't know for sure . . . but that seems likely."

Jake was appalled. In one week he had lost his family, become an international terrorist, been betrayed by his friends, and now he'd become addicted to a superpower drug that he had to keep using to stay alive.

He sat back down on the bed. "Why me? Why did you recruit me in the first place?"

"It's . . . complicated."

"Try me!" snarled Jake. There was an edge to his voice that had never been there before; something hinting at primal rage.

Basilisk took a tiny step back. Jake wondered if the supervillain was actually afraid of him.

"I raised objections with the Council over their methods of recruiting new talent and their insistence that any villain who wishes to cause chaos must first obtain a permit from them—just in case your plan clashes with somebody else's. They said, what is the point in robbing gold from a vault in Switzerland, only to find out some other villain is about to launch a death ray and destroy that country, and you with it, at the same time!"

Revelations

"They have a point," said Jake.

Basilisk raised his voice, causing Jake to jump. "It's a stupid system! Are you saying, if I want to take over the world I need a *permit* to do so? How villainous is *that*? It was bureaucratic red tape—an insult to chaos and mayhem!"

"So they threw you out?"

"I *left* their precious rules and guidelines behind. I had my own ambitions. Ambitions that require the removal of any interference from the Council."

"I still don't get what any of this has to do with me."

"You were one of those reasons I left, Hunter." Jake's surprise registered on his face, prompting a terse chuckle from Basilisk. "Are you familiar with the term 'feedback,' when a microphone or guitar is placed against the loudspeaker it is plugged into and you get an ear-piercing noise? That is because the same signal is caught in a loop. And each cycle produces a distorted version of the original."

Jake's favorite band, Ironfist, made constant use of feedback. Their guitarists were always posing in front of monolithic speakers. But the analogy made no sense to him.

"Look, stop talking in riddles and just tell me."

"There is part of you *already* in Villain.net, and by downloading from it you have created a feedback loop with your superpowers."

That made even less sense to Jake. "How can I be part of a Web site I've never seen before? That's crazy!"

"I was instrumental in creating Villain.net. Unfortunately for you we share something in common. Our DNA."

"That's impossible!"

"Believe me. You and I are related in ways that would stagger you."

"Related?" shrieked Jake in amazement.

The entire chamber suddenly shook. Stones skittered from the roof, and the furnishings bounced across the floor. At first Jake thought it was the volcano erupting, but then a whooping alarm sounded and a technician's voice shouted over the PA system.

"Intruders in base! Intruders in base! We're under attack!"

The Assault

Basilisk led the way through a series of corridors that were unfamiliar to Jake. He was completely lost, and was surprised when they suddenly ran into the hangar. The SkyKar sat right in front of them, partially blocking their view of the Core Probe in the center of the cavern.

Three technicians, still in plain white lab coats and toting small snub-nosed Uzi machine guns, crouched behind the Probe. They fired concentrated bursts across the hangar, taking care to avoid striking the nuclear warhead that was now mounted on top of the Probe. Their target was crouching behind a stack of metallic flight cases. The heady sound of staccato gunfire combined with the chunks of stone falling off the walls, reminded Jake that these were lethal bullets.

"Show yourself!" bellowed Basilisk.

A pair of silver energy bolts leaped from behind the cases and struck two of the gunmen. A fine crystalline coating smothered the men, freezing them in position— one with a bullet hanging midway from the barrel as though caught in amber.

Jake instinctively ducked behind the SkyKar, which he noticed was sporting additional damage from the combat.

"A superhero!" snarled Basilisk. He raised his hands and hurled an intense energy blast from his finger. The stack of flight cases exploded in fiery shrapnel that bounced against the walls.

"Not just anyone, Basilisk."

Jake heard a gasp from Basilisk before he recognized the voice himself. The mere thought of the name made his blood boil.

"Chameleon!" roared Basilisk.

"Now it's payback time," hissed the disembodied Chameleon.

Stillness descended over the chamber. The remaining technician lowered his gun, and nervously wiped the sweat from his brow as he peered into the shadows. Jake noticed two other technicians prone on the floor. They were not breathing. Plainly, even a superhero's morals were flexible when it came to eliminating potential threats.

Basilisk slowly approached the smashed pile of crates and peered into the darkness for any sign of the intruder. There was a sudden flurry of movement as Chameleon rushed past him, flipping the villain's hood off in the process. Jake just had time to see the hero was in his reptile form as he watched Chameleon skitter up the wall onto the dark ceiling, skirting around the circular exit hole.

Curiosity tore Jake's gaze back to Basilisk, who was pulling his hood back on. He had a fleeting glimpse of a pale head, with steel plates that folded into his skin.

Gunfire focused Jake's attention again and he saw the Uzi-toting technician fire at a shadow zipping across the roof. A silver blast struck the man, freezing him like a mannequin. Now Jake could see the intruder was directly above him—that is, until he dropped onto the roof of the SkyKar, which buckled under his weight right in front of Jake's nose.

Jake looked up at the yellow, scaly features of Chameleon peering down on him.

"I told you that you couldn't escape me, Hunter!"

"Why would I want to escape you when I'm going to *kill* you for what you did to my parents?" Jake snarled with such venom that Chameleon hesitated. Years of schoolyard instinct took over and Jake lashed out, hoping to send an energy blast at the freak. Instead, he felt a painful sensation at the tips of his fingers as catlike talons pushed from under his fingernails on both hands.

Chameleon bounded off the vehicle as Jake slammed his arms down on the car with such force he fractured the roof and his new claws tore through it like paper. Chameleon retreated up the wall like a gecko.

Basilisk circled around the opposite side of the cavern, trying to trap Chameleon between the two villains.

"You don't stand a chance, lizard breath! The boy is more powerful than you realize. And he wants you dead!"

"And I want *you* dead. What a predicament we have here," came the reply from the darkness. The hanging floodlights blinded Basilisk, preventing him from seeing beyond them.

Chameleon continued. "And I saved your family, Hunter. Saved them from the heartbreak you would have caused. They are happier because of what I did!"

Jake had been staring at the damage to the SkyKar, wondering what superpowers he'd been fed while unconscious, and how many. But Chameleon's taunts brought him back to the situation just as Basilisk fired a blast into the darkness above.

Rock exploded, but the flash was enough to briefly illuminate Chameleon as he reached a chunky electrical cable that branched out to each of the powerful floodlights on the ceiling. With a grunt of effort the hero tore the cable apart in a massive shower of sparks and the entire chamber was plunged into darkness and silence.

Jake's eyes picked out the faintest shaft of light coming from the open tunnel above them, which offered a glimmer of moonlight.

Then a ghostly green haze filled the room—or at least

that's what Jake first thought. It reminded him of TV news reports when they used night-vision cameras. It was the same feeling he'd had in Russia and now he could see Chameleon, hanging inverted on the ceiling, as a pulsing mass of electronic charges. It made the hero stand out against the blackness like bright stars on a clear night.

Jake could see Basilisk across the cavern, his arms outstretched as he fumbled blindly across the hangar, although the neon flare of his eyes could no doubt be seen by anybody. Chameleon had certainly picked him out as he raced across the ceiling and prepared to drop down on the unsuspecting villain.

"Basilisk! Above you!" bellowed Jake.

Basilisk heeded the words without hesitation and shot a bolt of energy blindly upward. Chameleon fell from the roof as the blast hit overhead. He crashed awkwardly onto the floor and rolled into a table as a chunk of the ceiling pulverized another workbench.

Jake saw Chameleon's shape waver, transforming back into that of the dark-haired young man, the reptilian skin morphing into normal clothing. Jake assumed this must be Chameleon's natural form, and the lizard transformation just one of his many powers. Chameleon looked around and spotted Jake. He too could see in the dark.

Chameleon raised his hands with a snarl and launched a fireball at Jake, which lit the cavern with flickering orange light. Jake ducked behind the SkyKar as it was hit with the force of a wrecking ball. The vehicle cannoned into him, and crushed him against the wall.

The brief illumination from the flames made Jake's vision revert to normal and was enough for Basilisk to get his bearings. He spun around and shot an enfilade of energy across the floor, tearing the ground from under Chameleon's feet. The hero was pitched backward, his feet arcing over his head as he slammed heavily onto a trestle table that cracked in two under the force of the impact.

"You'll die just like your partner!" roared Basilisk. "But first you can watch my operation unfold and know there is nothing you can do to stop it from happening!"

Jake grunted and pushed himself away from the wall, shrugging off the SkyKar, which rolled aside with a crunch of metal. The vehicle was aflame, filling the cavern with a dim light. Jake felt the muscles in his arms swell powerfully and the claws in his fingers retract. He registered that he must have some incredible strength to have pushed the heavy SkyKar.

He looked around the chamber and assessed the situation. Chameleon was lying on his back amid the wreckage of a workbench and seemed momentarily stunned.

Basilisk seemed more interested in delivering a monologue to the hero than killing him. He activated the small control panel on the side of the Core Probe. The machine hummed to life. The lasers energized, and the underside dome blazed to life as they focused their combined efforts on the dome's transparent surface. The dome began to glow, the superheated air around it becoming a haze.

"What are you doing?" shouted Jake. "This is not the plan!"

Jake was so absorbed by Basilisk's actions that neither of them noticed Chameleon stir, rubbing his head as he propped himself up on his elbow. He was aghast when he noticed Basilisk had powered up the machine.

"No! You'll kill us all!"

Basilisk barely had time to spin around before Chameleon unleashed a fireball that caught him full in the chest. Jake watched in horrified fascination as Basilisk was hurled some sixty feet across the cavern—and crunched into the wall, his cloak and hood ablaze. The fiend rolled on the ground trying to smother the flames, screaming as he did so.

Jake knew he should help Basilisk, but as he stepped forward, Chameleon spun around and targeted him with a fireball. Jake jumped straight up, still unsure which superpowers the doctor had cycled through his system. Was flight one of them?

Luck was with him. Jake soared like a rocket as the fireball struck the wall below him. He extended his hand in the hope he had some type of missile power, but cracked his head forcibly against the ceiling. He had not been looking where he had been flying and the impact knocked him out for a moment. Jake fell onto the flaming wreckage of the SkyKar. The chassis buckled, effectively cushioning his fall. The impact roused him to consciousness and he rolled off before he burned.

"Time to stop playing, Hunter," snarled Chameleon. "I would rather bring you in alive."

Dazed, Jake touched his head. His hair felt damp and sticky and when he pulled his hand away, it was covered in blood.

Chameleon took a step toward him, but hesitated as the noise from the machine increased. The dome was now blazing like a supernova and sending waves of heat that everybody could feel. The stone floor beneath the Probe was hissing and popping like fat in a pan.

"Basilisk!" shouted Chameleon. "Stop the machine!"

Jake knew he had to act quickly. With Chameleon's attention diverted, he sprang to his feet and slid one arm under the burning chassis of the SkyKar and the other around a bent window spar. He lifted the hulk with the minimum of effort. Chameleon shot a glance back at Jake, as the boy lugged the entire weight of something akin to a pickup truck over his head. He spat blood from a cut on his lip and glared at Chameleon.

"You took my family away from me! There's no way you live!" Jake felt hatred like he'd never felt before.

The Assault

An accumulation of betrayal and grief was pouring from him. Despite all his bluster, bullying, and obnoxious behavior, Jake had never thought he could kill. But his mind was now occupied with just one thought:

Kill Chameleon.

Bracing both feet apart, Jake grunted and hurled the burning SkyKar at the superhero. Chameleon was rooted to the spot as the flaming wreckage flew toward him. It was like being hit by a bus. The momentum swept Chameleon off his feet, and sent him crashing against one of the doors.

Jake stared at his handiwork, his heart pounding. Just one of Chameleon's legs could be seen jutting from the bottom of the wreckage. It twitched twice before falling still.

Jake swallowed hard. Had he just killed a superhero? He felt a tremor of guilt, but that was snubbed when he thought of the pain Chameleon had brought on him. The hero should never have messed with his family.

Jake glanced at the Core Probe as it began its descent, then sprinted across to Basilisk, who had doused the flames. Jake could see his arms were charred black, and a large portion of his cape and hood was burned away, although he still managed to keep his face covered. His breathing came in wheezing bursts.

"Are you hurt?"

"He caught me unprepared."

Jake helped him stand. The villain limped heavily on his right foot, and Jake moved around to take the weight off that side.

"We should get you to the hospital wing."

"No doubt the good doctor was evacuated the moment the alarms sounded, as were all nonessential personnel. I'll live. I am blessed with the gift of regeneration."

"What is that?"

"It's the ability to heal wounds very quickly. Although it's not what it used to be." Basilisk looked across at the still form of Chameleon pinned under the SkyKar. He grunted with satisfaction. "You did well. Splendid improvisation. Shame about my car, though."

"Stop the Core Probe," Jake said firmly.

Jake thought Basilisk was about to argue, but instead the arch-criminal nodded and, pushing Jake away, limped toward the machine. The intense heat did not seem to bother him. He selected two wires, a red and a blue, and pulled one free. The Core Probe's lasers powered down with a whistle, although the glass dome still glowed white-hot. Basilisk lovingly slid his hand across its cool upper surface.

"It is just as well it didn't launch. My Dutch friend had not yet programmed the correct drilling path to compensate for the Probe's extra payload. It would not do to miss its mark."

"I would have thought the earth's core was a pretty

big target." Basilisk said nothing. Jake shook his head and pointed to the console. "That's all you have to do? Pull out a wire to break the thing? It's not exactly sabotage-proof."

Basilisk pointed to the wire. "The blue one simply shuts the circuits down. If I had pulled the red it would have overloaded the machine and detonated the warhead instantly."

Jake felt uncomfortable with the thought. "You're not really going to detonate the warhead, are you? That's suicidal!"

"Remember this, Hunter. Idle threats fool nobody, and earn you no respect. When your back is against the wall you should use every weapon in your arsenal to escape with your life. Life is *the* most important asset you will ever have."

"But this entire plan will end both our lives! Is that why you started the Probe? Because your back was against the wall?"

"If I'm going down, then it's not going to be without a fight and certainly not alone." Basilisk limped toward the command center. "But I assure you, we shall survive."

Once again Jake felt his conscience tug at him. This was most definitely wrong. Despite the fact Jake had been instrumental in buying the nuclear warhead, he had hoped that Basilisk was bluffing and had no intention of detonating the bomb. But now he had seen firsthand that he had been wrong. Basilisk clearly had no regard for the world around him. He was obviously mad, and that sent a genuine ripple of fear through Jake as he followed him.

The command room was down to just three "essential" technicians who didn't seem in the least bit fazed by the loss of their companions. On-screen they had a satellite map of the island with two highlighted blips slowly moving in from the sea. Basilisk pointed to them and turned to Jake.

"You see that? That's an Enforcer task force. They are coming here because of you."

"Me?" said Hunter in surprise. "I think you mean 'us.'"

"Chameleon placed a tracer on your boot when you fought in Moscow. We removed it while you were unconscious, but by then it was too late. You led them here!"

Jake felt annoyed that somebody had found yet another way to use him. Basilisk turned to another computer terminal, where the Dutch drilling expert, Ruben Carlisse, was seated.

"Do it!" ordered Basilisk.

"You have to lift the veil of secrecy some time!" Ruben complained. "If you want the Core Probe to arrive at its target, then you must tell me exactly what kind of payload it is carrying!"

Jake frowned. Didn't the engineer know what madcap scheme he had been drafted into? He crossed over to the arguing men.

"The payload need not concern you," Basilisk muttered. "You have the measurements and the weight. That is all you need to make the calculations."

"No no no!" Ruben slammed his palms against the desk, his face flushing red. "When I agreed to this project I assumed it was a legitimate business case. Only when I met you did I realize there was something more devious going on. And now you tell me the Probe will be carrying a payload that will affect how fast the machine bores, how different densities of rock will alter its path, and how it will cope in the fluid magma beneath the mantle. If you want me to work, give me the facts or I leave!"

Jake decided to intervene. "It's a nuclear warhead."

Basilisk turned to Jake, seething with anger. Ruben froze, and for a moment Jake thought Basilisk had somehow paralyzed him. Then the engineer fell back in his chair, his voice softening.

"A nuclear bomb? Are you mad?"

"Madness is a matter of opinion," muttered Basilisk. "Get me those calculations."

"Do you realize what would happen if you detonated a bomb?"

Jake stared at Basilisk defiantly. "The earth will spin off its axis, scattering seasons, thawing the poles, and turning the deserts into oceans?"

Ruben frowned and shook his head. "No, not with a single warhead."

Jake breathed a sigh of relief, but he was almost afraid to believe what Ruben had just told him. "There's just the one." From Ruben's expression Jake suddenly had a bad feeling that yet another lie was about to be revealed.

Ruben licked his dry lips. "Detonating a nuclear warhead in a *volcanic* system, like this island, would set off a global chain reaction in *other* volcanoes."

Basilisk stepped back, as though encouraging Ruben to speak. Jake looked at the two men. "A volcanic system? But I thought you were going to send the Probe to the center of the earth and detonate it there?"

Basilisk shrugged. "You had to believe something. Why not that?"

Ruben continued. "The volcano system around the world is like the earth's pressure release and they're all linked together. Basically, when things get tight under the surface we have volcanic eruptions to ease pressure. Detonating a bomb in that system would cause a mass volcanic eruption across the world. If all the volcanoes explode simultaneously, that would cause earthquakes, tidal waves, and it would send massive amounts of ash into the atmosphere, blotting the sun. Effectively turning the world into night."

For a few seconds silence filled the command center. Then one of the technicians' mobile phones rang an irritatingly cheery tune. He had the good grace to silence it immediately.

Basilisk nodded. "Of course you are right. But I am only taking out *one* volcano. And to achieve maximum effect I need that Probe to be at a precise depth. Are you going to program the coordinates, as per our deal?"

Jake couldn't hold his temper in this time. "You lied to me again!"

"I did not! I told you the plan—"

"You told me a bluff. The demands, the money, weapons—it's all a big extravagant bluff. You're doing all this, ruining *my* life, just to destroy one single volcano? What's so special about it?"

Basilisk ignored Jake and placed a heavy hand on Ruben's shoulder. Ruben stared at the floor for a moment, wiping his palms against his shorts. Then he slowly stood and looked defiantly at Basilisk.

"No. I will not be part of this. I demand you let me leave immediately."

He took a step forward, but Basilisk shot a hand up against the man's chest to stop him.

"We have a contract." The tone in Basilisk's voice was menacing enough to prevent Jake from ranting again. "I am not an unreasonable man and appreciate we all make rash decisions in the heat of the moment. You have already calculated the densities of the rock?"

"Yes."

"And computed the tunneling time to our agreed detonation point in the volcanic chambers?"

Ruben hesitated as it dawned on him that there wasn't much use for him after all. Basilisk had come to the same conclusion.

"Then you have completed your task?"

A flicker of confidence crossed Ruben's face. "You still cannot do it without me. The cargo weight has been factored in, but the shape of this bomb you have attached could create drag on the Core Probe that would turn it off course. Then it would be pointless sending it down. So you listen to me, or I go to the authorities."

"Running the Core Probe off course is a minor risk, my friend. You have completed the contract. But I cannot permit you to run free to the authorities running your mouth."

Ruben gathered his nerves and managed to look defiant. "So what are you going to do? Kill me?"

"What an insightful idea."

Basilisk's palm shot around the man's throat and he effortlessly hoisted him off the ground. Ruben's feet swung free and both his hands gripped the fiend's wrist, fruitlessly clawing at the stone arm as he choked.

The Assault

With one hand Basilisk lifted the man so they were nose to nose. Then he pulled back his hood.

Jake could not see Basilisk's face. But what he could see was the back of a pale head that looked heavily burned. Patches of blond hair clung to the scalp, and the skin was pulled tight across the skull.

Ruben's eyes boggled in terror at the face he saw. His thrashing became wilder, his feet kicking Basilisk in the groin and chest, but the villain didn't flinch. Then, Jake heard a cracking sound like the noise ice cubes make when they rapidly melt in a drink. Ruben's face lost its color as he was petrified. In five seconds the Dutchman had been turned to stone from head to foot, silencing his screams. For an instant, Jake could just see the blue light of Basilisk's eyes reflected from the man's frozen face. Then Basilisk let go of the Ruben-statue and it shattered on the floor. Basilisk made a point of crushing several larger chunks under the heel of his boot.

Jake was aware that everybody in the room had stopped what they were doing and were staring at the execution in silence. As Basilisk spun around, everybody looked back at their work.

All except Jake. He gawked at Basilisk's unmasked face. It was scarred and disfigured. The eyes had no white, but were completely neon blue. But Basilisk had one unmistakable quality.

He looked just like Jake.

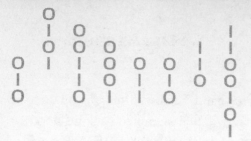

A Race to the End

The blaze in Basilisk's eyes cooled down. His face was pale and scarred; his skin had the texture of parchment, with small metal plates attached to it.

"How . . . how is this possible?" stammered Jake.

Basilisk drew in a deep breath; the wheezing had vanished along with the limp. His regeneration process was working.

"I told you all along, Hunter," he said in a low voice that was barely louder than a whisper. "It was in your blood."

Jake shook his head blankly, and took a step back as Basilisk advanced. Basilisk gestured between the two of them.

"You and I share the same DNA. Genetically there appears nothing to separate us. Any analysis of crime scenes would show that it was *you* who was there. Not me."

Jake had already been splashed across the news, and now it appeared that if the authorities ever managed to decrypt the video and audio ransom demand he'd recorded, they would have both his face and voice. And his DNA was all over who knew how many crime scenes. And it was all over the nuclear bomb.

"You've been using me as a scapegoat? All this time you were setting me up so that you could just turn me in and ride victoriously off into the sunset?"

Basilisk raised his hands to placate Jake. "I admit that was my original intention. Let my genetic twin get caught so that I could escape. Even the Council of Evil disapproved. And when they knew I was going to let you access the V-net system, they feared the worst, which is why I left. Creative differences. But instead of bringing the Web site down, you changed into something . . . unexpected."

"I should kill you right now like I did Chameleon. That would end this madness!" Jake advanced and was surprised to see Basilisk retreat a step.

"But things changed, Hunter. I got to see your potential. Downloading powers which had my—*our*—DNA in them, entwined you with Villain.net. You are absorbing all the powers at an incredible rate. Using them without training as though they were a natural extension of your body. That is unheard of. Now *you* are more important to me than this entire operation."

Jake hesitated. He wasn't convinced. Then again, Basilisk may be a liar, but he had yet to officially show his colors as a backstabber like Scuffer and the others.

And he was certainly no less aggressive than the apparent superhero Chameleon.

"Sir!" chimed a technician who was monitoring the large display screen. "The vehicles will be landing in several minutes! We've identified them as Navy Seal Sea Crawlers. There must be about thirty Enforcers in them."

Basilisk switched his gaze from the screen back to Jake. "If we don't act *now*, then in a few minutes those Enforcers will storm the base and put a stop to all I have created."

"I don't care. You need to tell me everything—now."

Basilisk sighed, and at least this time Jake could see the annoyed expression. "If they get in here, then you'll never know the full extent of your own story. Hunter, right now you have more power flowing through you than you imagine. Only you can go out there and stop them. Then we will have time to talk."

"There it was again," thought Jake, "more orders. More bullying and being told what to do." For a moment he wished he were back at school. Then he'd have the power to pick on those weaker than him.

Suddenly Jake paused. Common sense dictated you wouldn't pick on somebody stronger than yourself. Unless that person didn't realize they were stronger than you.

Was he stronger than Basilisk?

A Race to the End

The villain had just said that Jake didn't know his own power. He'd made no attempt to physically threaten Jake at any time, nor had he threatened to harm Jake's family to coerce him, unlike the "good guys." The more Jake thought about it, the more clearly he saw that he had willingly played along with events, never daring to challenge Basilisk, no matter what deep waters he had led him into.

With sudden clarity, Jake realized that *he* was afraid of Basilisk. Frightened of upsetting the balance in their relationship just by simply challenging him. Jake was experiencing the same fear that stopped the kids Jake bullied from punching back. He wasn't made of metal; a firm left hook would double him over just like anybody else. It was fear that made those dorky kids curl up and take their punishment.

And now Jake was one of those kids. He was a victim of bullying.

"No!" he heard himself bellow. The force of the words made Basilisk hesitate. "I want to know exactly who you are! And no more stupid cover stories!"

Basilisk seemed to realize that he had pushed Jake too far. He began pacing once again and occasionally cast a glance at the screen. "You really want to know who I am? Do you think that will help you in any way?"

"Humor me."

Basilisk sighed. "I have been walking this planet for

many years. Centuries, in fact. You could say that I'm immortal."

"You can't die?"

"Yes, I can. But I found a method of cheating aging by moving from incarnation to incarnation. It was a power I had. A gift. Having the accumulated knowledge of the centuries has made me quite a scientist, and like all scientists I specialized. I chose genetics. That allowed me to study my powers and discover what was really happening. It was in the nineteen sixties when I found out how my incarnations actually worked."

Basilisk paused, reflecting back on his memories of the time. Jake tried to imagine Basilisk in the 1960s with bell-bottoms and long hippie hair. The thought almost raised a smile.

Basilisk continued. "Genetic studies were one of my key inputs into Villain.net. I told you that we improvised in some areas. I fine-tuned the site's ability to alter human genetic code so that a host would be capable of storing and using the superpowers. But the Hero Foundation had cracked the problem in a much more efficient way. They never suffered the side-effect issues we had in our version. But I came up with a quick solution that seemed to work. I developed a method of using the regeneration aspects of my own DNA strands to absorb the malign effects."

Jake nodded in understanding. He was impressed with

his new mental gymnastics, and wondered if he had superintelligence. "So when somebody downloaded a faulty power, your own DNA would repair it within the person's body, and stop any side effects?"

"Very good. However, since you and I have the same DNA sequence it formed a feedback loop when *you* used Villain.net. It made your powers much stronger than anybody else's, including the Prime's original powers. But it came at a cost. Your body is breaking down from trying to contain the excessive energy, and, without constant exposure to the power source, you'll wither away. Because of the feedback, the regeneration doesn't work with you."

"So you've killed me!" snapped Jake bitterly.

"You misunderstand, Hunter. Nobody knew this would happen. The Council suspected it might kill you, but being able to amplify the strength of your powers is something unforeseen. Something that *both* sides desperately want. Chameleon is not too concerned about stopping that bomb. He is more interested in *you*. Let me assure you that you have no friends on either side right now. Except me."

That thought made Jake feel hollow inside.

"I chose you at your birth and have been watching you for a long time, subtly guiding your actions from afar in the hope you would grow up to be a warrior and not a coward like the rest of your friends."

This was a lot of information for Jake to process. So he was unique in being able to amplify his powers, but that still didn't explain why they originally shared the same DNA. What had Basilisk done?

"Sir! We're running out of time! They've begun to land," wailed the technician.

"If they are not stopped—," he threw Jake a meaningful glance "—then evacuate the base and activate the self-destruct." He turned his attention back to Jake. "Your choice, Hunter."

"What do you mean, since birth? Why me?"

Basilisk was apparently losing patience but he calmed himself down and fixed his gaze on Jake.

"As I said, to cheat death I have the ability to absorb DNA. Just a small sample is enough to rejuvenate my body and mind. I was dying. I needed to make a genetic regeneration quickly. Did your parents ever tell you the circumstances of your birth?"

"My mom gave birth to me on the way to the hospital."

"Fortuitously for me, I was in the area. The younger the DNA I can clone, the longer I live. A newborn baby is much better than a teenager or an adult. Gives me a few more years. A little knockout gas took care of your parents for a few moments while I stole DNA from your wrist." Jake looked at his wrist where he had had a circular dimple since birth. "Sorry, I was in a rush. The side effect of genetic rejuvenation is that I take on the physical characteristics of the donor—hence the family resemblance. I shall be like this until it is time for me to change once more, which will be very soon as you can tell from my appearance. Time is once more running out for me. Think of me as a genetic vampire, if you will. But I make a point of looking after my genetic counterpart, so I watched you and molded your development so you became strong and independent."

"You made me callous and bitter?" snarled Jake. "Are you trying to say you made me into the kid that picks on everybody?"

"I certainly engineered it, yes. Your friends are the true unintelligent bullies. But I molded you to be a *thinker* and a *leader*. Why else would somebody from such a loving family become such a monster?" He said the last with a tinge of sarcasm.

"You ruined my life!"

"No. I gave you chances you would never have experienced!" He jabbed a finger at the intruders on the screen. "They are the people who ruined your life, made you a wanted man and took away your family's memories! The people who think they are doing a good deed. As they say, the road to hell is paved with good intentions. You should be stopping *them*!"

Jake wanted nothing more than to lunge at Basilisk and beat the evil creep to a pulp. But that would still leave questions unanswered.

"You've done nothing but lie to me!"

"Sometimes I had to manipulate the truth."

"You told me your name was Scott Baker, and that you were from Australia. Lies!"

"With each regeneration I needed a genuine identity to make my way around the world. I sometimes pick my identities from the deceased, acquiring their legal papers, bank accounts, that sort of thing. Otherwise, where would I put my money? Would you trust a bank run by villains? Sometimes lies are easier than the truth. But it is no lie that we have to stop those Enforcers from interfering. Please, Hunter. Do this."

Jake hesitated. He was cornered and had no intention of allowing the Enforcers to capture him. Glaring at Basilisk he stalked from the command center without saying a further word, and slid his gloves on.

His mind was racing as he sprinted down the corridor. He wanted to cry at the injustice of it all—crying would be something he hadn't done for a long time, but wouldn't be appropriate right now. His thoughts turned to self-preservation. Could the feedback process be reversed? Then he thought about the fact that both heroes and villains wanted to experiment on him. Where did that leave Jake?

What do you call somebody stuck in the middle?

Jake entered the hangar and prepared to launch himself vertically through the hole in the roof. Something caught his attention: the SkyKar had been moved, and Chameleon's body was nowhere to be seen.

"No!" shouted Jake. He ran to the spot and looked around. There was a little blood, but no sign of where the hero had run to. Well, that was a problem for Basilisk right now. He just hoped he could get to Chameleon before Basilisk did.

Jake focused on the task at hand. He had to stop the beach attack. With a warming surge as the powers flowed through him, Jake launched himself skyward.

Basilisk glared at the display screen as a second blip appeared in the center of the island: it was Jake. Basilisk was annoyed at himself for revealing so much to Jake so soon. But at least he still hadn't revealed his *ultimate* intentions and so still had some control over the boy— and control was something he needed. He was beginning to regret selling his last pair of power-dampening handcuffs to Doc Tempest on his last visit. They would be handy now. If Jake was ever to find out the true extent of his mutated powers . . . Basilisk shivered. That thought was too dark even for *him* to consider.

"Incoming transmission," shouted one of the technicians.

"On-screen," commanded Basilisk.

The satellite map shrank away to a corner of the screen

as the new transmission took over. Eight unusual figures appeared: the Council of Evil.

One spoke in a sibilant voice. "We have discovered your true plan, Basilisk! The real one, not the lies you've been spinning to the world's governments! This is madness!"

"Doc Tempest betrayed you!" said a woman's voice with a hint of glee. "He told us everything. Stabbed you in the back so he could have an official permit for his own plan."

Basilisk smirked. "You think I was mad enough to turn the earth into a wasteland? What use is that to me? I intend to blow Villain.net and your pathetic Council off the face of the planet!"

"You'll never get away with this!"

"I already have. And being one of the few people who knows your headquarters lies in an extinct volcano, I finally discovered a method of breaching all of your state-of-the-art defenses. No missile attacks, no swarming armies. I will just simply blow your lair apart from under your feet as you cower in terror!"

"Once again, you threaten to destroy the world!"

"I have taken precautions to ensure my lair was constructed at the precise point on the volcanic network to maximize the destruction of your base. My engineers have worked tirelessly to block magma channels in order to prevent other volcanoes from erupting. The earth's pressure will build to such intensity that your extinct volcano will be magically resurrected. Then, by using Hunter's amplified powers, all I have to do is take over Hero.com and I will control the only superpowers left. Nothing in the universe can stop me!"

Basilisk was swelling with his own self-importance. He stabbed a button and killed the connection with the Council. He turned to a technician. "Launch the Probe!"

Nothing happened. Then Basilisk noticed that three of the technicians were stuck fast to their seats by large globules of sticky glue that bound their arms and covered their mouths to silence them.

Basilisk turned to see that a fourth technician was standing close by and pointing a resin-rifle at him. Basilisk's puzzlement vanished as the technician's clothing and skin rippled into a vaguely reptilian form, and then into that of a young man dressed in black. Chameleon.

"The Council made such a pleasant diversion, didn't it? Your insanity ends here."

"This must be the same thrill a lion feels as it stalks its prey," thought Jake as he felt the sand crunching under his boots. The figures in the trees were picked out like Christmas lights in his enhanced vision. They had nowhere to run. Black smoke drifted behind him

from the damaged Sea Crawlers, polluting the clear tropical air.

The ground shook; he looked up. Beyond the cowering Enforcers a spectacular plume of red lava spewed from the lip of the volcano.

Jake looked at the Enforcers, who were twisting their necks between the erupting volcano behind and the ominous figure of death on the beach. Basilisk had said they were the real threat, but looking at them now he realized they were just normal men, trying to do a job without the aid of superpowers. Unlike Chameleon, who hid behind his powers.

"Who cares about these Enforcers?" thought Jake. They posed no threat. The erupting volcano signified that Basilisk had just launched the Core Probe and its nuclear payload.

Jake decided that it was time to take matters into his own hands.

The Enforcers cowered as Jake ran toward them. They were expecting another barrage of superpowers. But their assailant rose into the air and zoomed over the treetops, heading toward the eruption.

For once he was going to do some good. He was going to stop Basilisk.

Basilisk repeatedly slammed Chameleon's head against

the control panel with such ferocity he was drawing gloopy green blood. He had the superhero in a viselike grip amid the trashed command center.

"I should have dealt with you a long time ago!" Basilisk roared in his face.

Chameleon fired the resin-rifle at Basilisk in the hope it would restrain him, but instead the expanding glue-balls ricocheted from an invisible shield. Basilisk had retaliated with a blast that sent Chameleon soaring through the massive screen in an explosion of sparks and plasma fluid.

The three technicians, who were stuck to their chairs, still had the use of their feet and rolled their chairs toward the nearest exit.

Chameleon counterattacked by hurling fireballs across the room, decimating several computer banks. Basilisk had dived aside and activated the Core Probe's remote launch sequence before Chameleon had a handle on what was happening. The superhero leaped onto Basilisk's back to pull him away, but was too late.

The entire hangar started to tremble as the Core Probe thrust itself earthward. Rock bubbled and melted away as the device slowly lowered itself. It quickly vaporized the ground in its path and after a few feet it pierced a small magma chamber under the volcano. But that was enough to initiate a local eruption. The entire base shook as the volcano erupted far above the surface.

Basilisk and Chameleon struggled, limbs locked together on the floor as they rolled through chunks of burning control panel. Basilisk was proving to be the stronger of the two and twisted Chameleon around, gripping him tightly across the jaw.

Chameleon tried to shapeshift as Basilisk crushed his head repeatedly against the panels. But no matter what shape he took, Basilisk's grip was relentless. He forced Chameleon to face him.

"No!" pleaded Chameleon as the intensity of Basilisk's soulless blue eyes increased. Chameleon could feel the warmth being sucked from his body and his limbs becoming stiffer. His skin took on an unhealthy sheen and his face felt immobile, as if mud had rapidly dried across it. He was being petrified, and the experience was horrendous.

Basilisk felt a heavy weight suddenly slam into his back. The momentum propelled him clear of Chameleon. The pallor left Chameleon's face, but he was still weak. Both he and Basilisk looked up to see Jake standing in the doorway ready to hurl another energy blast, and oblivious to the burning wreckage around him.

"Stop the Probe!" Jake shouted.

Basilisk was on his knees. He held up his hand in a

pitiful gesture. "No, Hunter. You don't understand. It's not what you think—"

"Stop the Probe, *now*!" repeated Jake. A humorless grin filled his face. "Stop it, Basilisk, or you'll suffer the same fate I have planned for lizard boy."

"I can't stop the Probe! The planet will *not* be destroyed. I've already told you that was never the plan! I just thought I could strip countries of their armies and extort some money as an afterthought."

"Then what's the warhead for?"

Basilisk spoke rapidly. "To bring down the Villain.net system and the Council of Evil along with it. Then, with the world's armies at my disposal, I would have finally been able to eliminate the superheroes from this world and every country would have been defenseless against me . . . I mean *us*!"

Jake hesitated. Why had Basilisk not told him about this before? Surely that was not as bad as destroying the world?

Gasping, Chameleon spoke. "Hunter, it's true. If he brings down the Council, then he can also destroy the V-net system."

"You shut up!" snarled Jake. "I still have you to deal with. You took everything away from me. Left me with nothing!"

Chameleon pressed on, almost babbling. "He will have unlimited access to all of those powers. If he were to

amplify them through you, then there would be no stopping him! *He* would become the most powerful person on the planet, not you. And pumping them through you would wear you away until you were dead."

Jake hesitated. He'd expected Chameleon to plead for his life. "If I let him," Jake retorted. He was no longer going to let Basilisk dictate the course of his life.

"You won't have a choice, Hunter," Chameleon croaked.

Basilisk tried to stand, but couldn't. He slowly dragged himself over to Chameleon.

"Silence!" bellowed Basilisk.

But Chameleon pushed on. "I know you want me dead, Hunter, but I'm trying to save your life here! Think about it! What would happen if Villain.net failed?"

Jake frowned. A moment ago, he thought he had been saving the world, but now the person he hated the most was telling him that his actions would actually defend a stupid Web site that Basilisk had been instrumental in creating. If Villain.net crashed, so what? He would lose his powers, and . . . the thought struck him like a lightning bolt.

He would die.

Basilisk had said as much. Jake's body craved the power surge offered by Villain.net. Basilisk had made him an addict, as dependent as the drug users that his schoolteachers constantly ranted about. And now Basilisk was willing to sacrifice Jake as a pawn in his twisted game.

Jake let out a roar so full of anger it took him by surprise. He threw his hands forward and familiar green streamers lashed out and struck Basilisk hard in the chest. The radioactive force burned across the villain's skin. Basilisk staggered backward. Jake was experiencing a gut-wrenching vehemence that he had never felt before. He wasn't finished with him yet.

"I'm tired of your lies! You've betrayed me, just like Scuffer and the others!"

Jake shifted his balance forward and shot into the air just as Basilisk got to his feet. Jake smashed into him with such a mighty force that he yanked Basilisk off the ground. They powered across the room, straight into the shaking wall, with the impetus of a jackhammer. Jake dropped to his feet. Basilisk was groggy and was still supported upright by the indentation he had created when he battered the wall. Jake flexed his razor-sharp claws and pulled his fist back to strike.

"That's not the way, Hunter!" Chameleon shouted, slowly climbing to his feet. "Killing him will solve nothing."

"It'll make me feel a whole lot better. Then you're next!"

"That means you'll be leaving the Core Probe active.

Stopping *that* is the only way you'll stay alive. You have no time to kill either of us."

Chameleon was right. Jake hesitated, then realized that Chameleon had just saved Basilisk's life. There was a sudden crack above them and a chunk of the ceiling gave way. Lava poured through it like a fiery waterfall. The air rippled from the intense heat, and the molten rock formed a thin curtain between Jake and Chameleon.

"We don't have time for this, Hunter. None of us has protection from being consumed by lava! Not even you."

The room shuddered more violently and the lava began to pool on the floor, spreading with the consistency of thick porridge. Jake squinted at the superhero.

"We're not finished, Chameleon."

Then he sprinted toward the door.

It was almost impossible to run in a straight line; the base was shaking so violently that Jake was pinballed against the walls of the corridor until he entered the cavern.

It was like entering a furnace. The far wall glowed red as magma flowed under the thin veneer of rock; it was only a matter of time before it all broke through. Already thin streams of lava poured through cracks in the ceiling. Molten rock slowly edged toward the wide borehole in the floor that the Core Probe had left behind. If the lava started to flow into the hole before he got into it, Jake knew there was no way he would be able to enter it and stop the Probe. He'd wasted precious time venting his rage against Basilisk, and now he could not afford to hesitate any longer. He took a running jump and dived headfirst down the Core Probe's tunnel.

There was very little room for maneuver in the tunnel, and the walls were red-hot from the Probe's passing. He zipped through an empty magma cave, the flow having erupted outside, and he dived back into the opposite borehole. The machine had gained substantial speed as it burrowed through the igneous rock. Jake activated his enhanced sight so he could see the Probe below. The heat prickled his skin all over and was beginning to penetrate through his jeans. Jake thought it must be like standing inside an oven. If he activated his radioactive power he would be resistant to the heat, but then ran the risk of being unable to grab the Probe and stop it, as his hand would just melt through the metal casing.

The Probe was now several feet below him. Jake acrobatically flipped around and landed on his feet, then maneuvered his legs to straddle the nuclear bomb strapped to the center. Basilisk's technicians had thoughtfully attached a small electronic counter to the bomb.

He had little over a minute.

"How do you defuse a nuclear bomb?" he said aloud. Then he remembered the wire Basilisk had pulled. Jake's fingers scrabbled for the only two wires that ran from the side of the machine into the warhead. He examined them and his heart sank.

They were both black. That is, the red and blue wires were indistinguishable through his tinted super-vision. It was as though he'd been struck color-blind.

"No!" he yelled and tried to will the power away. But it was no good. If he pulled the wrong wire the bomb would detonate between his legs.

He placed his hands around the warhead and pulled. The metal spars securing it groaned a little, but held tight. Jake tugged again, but his legs were shaking from the constant motion of the descent. It was like trying to lift something in a plummeting elevator.

The Core Probe gave a final shudder as it punctured a huge subterranean cavern—and was suddenly free-falling with Jake perched on top.

The cavern floor was a massive river of rolling magma that streamed from an opening in one wall and vanished through another with a rumble that numbed his ears. The entire vista was illuminated by the hellish red glow of the flowing rock, and the incredible heat seared his skin and burned his hair and eyebrows. If the Core Probe's heat shields had not been taking the brunt of the heat from below, then Jake was sure he would fry to death. An acrid burning smell assaulted his nose, and Jake felt it begin to bleed from the heat.

Without conscious thought, he launched himself into flight as the Probe dropped through the cavern—supporting it in midair above the magma river. His superior strength prevented him from dropping the Probe, but his flying power wasn't generating enough lift.

He was at a stalemate.

If he dropped the Core Probe into the magma, it wouldn't melt, but would continue its course downward and Jake would be unable to follow. But conversely, he didn't have the power to pull the Probe out.

Jake glanced at the countdown and resisted the urge to panic.

He looped one arm under the warhead and as soon as he had freed his other hand, he felt the weight of the entire device pull him toward certain death.

Jake flexed his claws and swiped them hard at the metal brace securing the warhead. Sparks flew and it felt as though his fingernails were being torn from their sockets. However, when he looked, he had managed to snag a chunk of metal away. The Probe dropped lower; the cutting dome was now touching the surface of the magma.

Jake's eyes stung from the heat and fumes. He struck again and one of the spars snapped. The Probe dropped farther into the volcano and liquefied rock spat at him. A tiny piece of molten rock caught the sole of his boot and hissed through the rubber.

Jake was a foot and a half away from the magma now, and with every ounce of strength he swung at the remaining strut. His claws severed the metal and the Core Probe dropped into the fiery liquid with a spurt of flame, the warhead now cradled under his arm.

Without the additional weight Jake shot upward like a cork underwater. The narrow Probe tunnel rushed past his ears just as lava started to trickle in from the hangar above.

Without stopping, Jake zoomed out of the hole in the hangar's floor and through the entrance tunnel in the ceiling.

He shot out of the ground just as the volcano erupted again. Part of the cone wall collapsed at an angle, spewing lava into the entrance of the base and across the jungle. Wildfires erupted across the island, but Jake had no time to marvel at the spectacle.

A mile above the island he drew to a stop. He was holding a nuclear warhead in his hand—with less than fifteen seconds on the countdown—and no way to stop it.

Jake had nothing to lose. He couldn't fly fast enough to outrun a nuclear explosion. Instead he willed a radioactive charge through his body and into his hands. His hands started to glow an unearthly green. The warhead's outer skin began to melt under his radioactive hands. The volcano spat another volley of lava into the sky, which fountained not far from Jake.

He could feel the warhead vibrate as the electronic ignition activated the fusion processes. He increased the pressure on the warhead, gouging his fingers in deep. Then he grunted, using every ounce of strength . . .

. . . and tore the warhead in half.

Sophisticated components and radioactive substances half-melded together under his mighty radioactive grip, flew in opposite directions, and harmlessly dropped into the ocean.

Jake whooped with delight and dived low, performing a victory roll. Jubilant, he skimmed the whitecaps around him, enjoying the gentle sea spray that cooled and refreshed him. With the warhead gone, Villain.net was saved.

He wasn't going to die.

All he had to do now was face Basilisk and Chameleon, if they hadn't torn each other apart.

Vengeful thoughts slipped from his mind as he felt a

sudden weakness—as if all the energy had seeped from his body. Jake plummeted into the warm waters.

His superpowers had just expired.

Panic seized him. The island beach was not too far away, but the island itself was on fire. Lava oozed down the volcano's flanks and hit the ocean with a loud hiss and massive plumes of white steam.

Jake spotted a clear patch of beach shielded from the lava streams and paddled weakly toward it.

It took all his strength to drag himself out of the water and across the white sand. He lay limp, facedown, and slipped into unconsciousness.

Jake looked at the bare stone walls with a blank expression. A table stood in front of him, on which he rested his shackled hands. The small interrogation room had a pair of Enforcer guards standing armed and alert on either side of the only door.

Chameleon, in his natural guise as a young man, sat opposite.

Jake had a vague memory of people landing on the beach and the rhythmic thump of helicopter rotors. He had seen Chameleon's face, but thought it was just part of a feverish dream. Then he had woken in a small cell with a narrow window through which stabbed a lone finger of sunlight.

A Race to the End

He was now a prisoner of Diablo Island Penitentiary, and Chameleon was taking great delight in taunting him.

"You should get a medal," said Chameleon. "You stopped a disastrous plan."

"Then let me go," said Jake quietly, although he already knew that was never going to happen.

Chameleon shook his head. "You'd only try and kill me. And that would land you right back here, wouldn't it?"

Jake couldn't deny it. All he had done from the start of the interview was threaten Chameleon, until he eventually shut up when he realized the futility of it. He'd bide his time instead.

"Your part in Basilisk's evil plans is undeniable. Since he miraculously escaped from that island, you're even more valuable to us."

"You let him go?" Jake said, incredulous.

"He escaped. I pursued him and thought I had him cornered. Then he vanished. He was too weak to have used his powers. I suspect an accomplice rescued him."

Jake's interest was tweaked. Who could have saved Basilisk? Surely not Doc Tempest—he had betrayed him.

"We found your three friends in Moscow. They had nothing nice to say about you. In fact, we're still trying to fathom *what* it was that you did to Warren Feddle.

What do you call him? Ah yes, Scuffer. You mutated him almost beyond recognition. And he's *very* eager to get his hands on you. An encounter I would strongly advise against. We have no idea what we'll do with him."

Jake scowled. So Scuffer had survived whatever he'd done to him? He should pay the traitors a little visit, with his superpowers of course, once he got out of here. It seemed all of Jake's enemies were not only alive, but a whole lot freer than he was.

"But that is all irrelevant compared to your true value." Chameleon took a sip of water from his glass, and absently shot his tongue out across his lips. "Amplifying the powers held on Hero.com. Now that is something truly special. And until we learn how to harvest that power, you will continue your residence here as our . . . uh . . . guest. Until the Enforcers can convene a trial. Then you'll be our prisoner, won't you?"

Chameleon smiled at him. Jake swore as the guards pulled him out, but without superpowers he was just an average kid, unable to resist the huge men. They threw him roughly into his cell and slammed the door shut. Multiple locks clicked in place, and one of the guards brushed a smudge from the nameplate on the cell door, which read, "THE HUNTER."

* * *

A Race to the End

Jake lay on his hard bed rubbing the marks left by the cuffs. He had not accessed any superpowers for several days and felt nauseous and weak. The medical staff had given him some pills that had kept him going, but Jake knew that even if they opened all the doors, he would not have the strength to walk out.

Once again he considered the line between hero and villain, but it was complicated. Basilisk was a villain, willing to detonate a nuclear bomb to bring down *other* villains, and Chameleon was a hero who had not hesitated to wipe his existence from his family's memories and showed no mercy to Basilisk's men when he had killed them.

Jake had been used by Chameleon to track down Basilisk, and also used by Basilisk to try and destroy the Council of Evil. And now the good guys were using Jake as a guinea pig.

He hated both sides. It seemed the only true line of justice lay with him alone. He promised himself that he would never be used again, and if there were any power and glory to be had, it would be solely his. He would not stop plotting to get out of this prison, and then he would track down *both* sides and make them pay for their actions.

They'd wish they had never heard the name Jake Hunter.

Jake lay back and savored the thoughts of revenge. As

he did so he noticed something solid was tucked under his pillow. He reached underneath and slid out a small mobile phone. He blinked in surprise.

There was a single text message waiting for him.

With a frown, Jake opened it. As he read, a broad smile crossed his lips.

The future suddenly promised to be *very* interesting. . . .

Coming soon, more action-packed adventures in the Villain.net series and Hero.com anti-series:

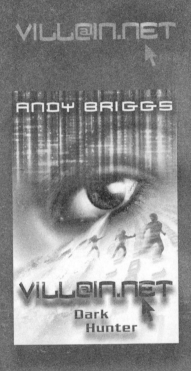

Available January 2010

THE WORLD IS YOURS
FOR THE TAKING!

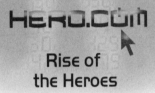

Frozen

The C-130 transport plane bucked against the invisible eddies that swirled around the aircraft 30,000 feet above the earth. More commonly known as a Hercules, the aircraft was the workhorse of the air force—but it had not been designed to take the kind of punishment that was hammering it now.

The malevolent storm had appeared from blue skies. Snow pelted the craft and choked the four powerful engines—one of which was still aflame from the missile impact—forcing it rapidly to lose airspeed and precious altitude. Below, the bleak continent of Antarctica beckoned to the Hercules' passengers with a subzero embrace.

Inside, two twelve-year-old boys—Toby and Pete—gripped the safety harnesses bolted to their jump seats, their knuckles white as the plane belly flopped. Any items not secured jumped into the air and remained there, held in a curious state of zero gravity as they nose-dived toward the earth.

Toby thought he was going to be sick for sure.

Frozen

Having watched countless documentaries on TV he remembered the term *parabola*: NASA flew planes toward the earth to simulate zero gravity. The planes were affectionately known as "Vomit Comets." And that's exactly how he felt now, feeling the bile rise in his throat.

He also remembered seeing that they would have about forty seconds of this nauseating feeling before the plane crashed into the ground. And after everything that had happened this week, he was pretty sure they wouldn't survive *that*.

All these thoughts flitted through Toby's mind in a second. He smashed open the restraining clip on his safety harness and floated out into the cargo area of the plane like he'd seen astronauts do on television.

Pete watched Toby free-float out and unbuckled his own belt to join him. Unable to precisely control his movements, Toby floated upside down, the inverted perspective disorienting him even more.

Thirty seconds to impact . . .

"We have to open the rear doors!" yelled Toby over the monstrous droning of the Allison Turboprop engines.

Pete looked around frantically. "The release switch is automated. It's in the cockpit."

"Shoot!" cried Toby.

They both knew there was no time to break into

the fortified cockpit and override the mechanical Drone Pilot.

Twenty-five seconds.

Toby kicked himself away from the bulkhead and soared toward the rear of the aircraft, steadying himself as he flew over pallets held in place with canvas webbing. He knew once they opened the door the supply pallets would create an additional problem.

Pete tried to use his arms to swim through the air; instead he revolved uselessly on the spot.

Toby cried over to him. "I can't do this! This is your area of expertise!"

Pete threw out a hand and steadied himself by catching the pallet webbing.

"Open the doors and use the pallets to spring out!" cried Toby.

That was the problem with flying; it was difficult to do if you were plummeting. You needed a springboard to push yourself upward. Even with superpowers, physics always butted in its unwelcome nose.

Twenty . . .

Pete laboriously heaved himself over to Toby. Both boys planted their feet against the pallets, coiled for action.

Pete removed his glasses—he had learned his lesson long ago—and focused on the rear cargo door that opened like a jaw under the Hercules' tail section.

Frozen

BAM! A concentrated beam of blue energy leaped from his eyes and blew the cargo door into twisted metal fragments. Frigid winds sucked at the aircraft's contents.

The sudden loss of pressure pulled the contents of the craft out with teeth-jarring speed. The pallets vaulted under their feet, rocketing the boys out into the blizzard. Inertia pushed them flat against the boxes underfoot, but both boys knew they had to push upward; otherwise they would simply crash into the ground with the rest of the aircraft.

Using every part of their remaining strength, they pushed—and suddenly they found themselves flying up, away from the aircraft and its cargo of supply pallets—

And toward the jagged mountains!

No sooner had they taken flight than the Hercules smashed forcibly into the side of one of the mountains. Pete's mental countdown had not taken into account the fact that the ground had swept up in the form of the Neptune Mountain Range to meet them.

The Hercules transport erupted into a vivid orange fireball. Twenty free-falling pallets impacted into the inferno seconds later. Toby could feel the flames licking his heels, but he urged himself to fly faster, throwing out both arms before him, in case that helped. From the corner of his eye, he saw Pete banking downward, away from the fireball's path. Toby lost no time in joining him.

They arced around and down in a flight path that a military jock would term a "yo-yo maneuver." Within seconds the steeply sloping, icy flanks of the mountain were underneath them and the Hercules was no longer visible in the storm.

The cold bit hard, sapping Toby's energy even through the multilayered thermal gear that covered almost every inch of him. He knew he had no choice but to land firmly on the mountain slope, or risk dropping from the sky and rolling the rest of the way downhill. A quick glance confirmed Pete was thinking the same.

Toby pivoted so he was no longer aiming headfirst down the mountain. He slowed, dropping the last few feet to the ground. He fell on all fours to keep his balance, and sank to his knees and elbows. Pete landed next to him. Already the driving blizzard had coated them with a layer of frost.

Pete's teeth chattered. "That . . . was a new experience, huh?"

Before Toby could reply, a noise got his attention. It was bass-heavy, countering the wind's whistle. The ground beneath them shook; with a feeling of dreadful realization, Toby turned his gaze uphill.

The flaming carcass of the aircraft was sledging down the hill, and gaining momentum with every second.

"Watch out!" Toby screamed.

Frozen

He had no time to push his friend aside. Instead he could only leap sideways with the very last of his energy.

His face was buried in the snow as he landed, and the world shook around him as the burning twisted debris thundered past like a runaway train. He remained motionless as, seconds later, he was pelted with smaller debris that bounced off his protective gear. Toby was sure that had he not been wearing the multiple layers, a jagged piece of shrapnel would have cut him open.

The ground stopped trembling and the driving wind howled some more. Toby picked himself up and looked around wildly.

Pete was gone.

"Pete! Where are you?"

Panic seized him, overriding the permeating chill. He staggered forward.

"Pete! Answer me! Please?"

He looked around hopelessly, and then dropped to his knees. With every ounce of self-control, he stopped himself from crying; tears would freeze over his eyeballs in the -58° Fahrenheit atmosphere and would no doubt blind him.

If the aircraft had hit Pete then he would definitely be dead. Pete's current range of superpowers would do nothing to save him from being crushed by a flaming aircraft.

Dead. Maybe like Lorna, Emily . . . and his mother.

Toby shook the dark thoughts from his mind and assessed his situation. It was almost as bleak. He was two thousand miles away from the nearest civilization, which was located on the tip of Argentina, trapped at over a thousand feet on the snow-covered peak. Hurricane-strength winds promised to spirit him away if he dared fly again—not that he had the strength.

His best friend was probably dead. His sister and her friend had been caught by henchmen, and a madman held his mother captive: an unspeakably evil villain who had demolished Fort Knox.

And it seemed Toby was the only person who could now save the world from disaster.

Talk about a bad week.

Toby reflected on how the last seven days had transformed their lives beyond imagination. In one moment he and his friends had turned from regular kids into superheroes. The innocence of their youth had been stripped raw.

Everything had changed the day they chanced on the source of their extraordinary powers. . . .

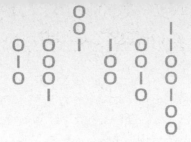

Andy Briggs was born in Liverpool, England. Having endured many careers, ranging from pizza delivery and running his own multimedia company to teaching both IT and filmmaking (though not all at the same time), he eventually remembered the constant encouragement he had received at an early age about his writing. That led him to launch himself on a poor, unsuspecting Hollywood. In between having fun writing movie scripts, Andy now has far too much fun writing novels.

He lives in a secret lair somewhere in the southeast of England—attempting to work despite his two crazy cats. His claims about possessing superpowers may be somewhat exaggerated. . . .

CAN'T GET ENOUGH OF SAVING THE WORLD?
DISCOVER THE WORLD OF THE SEEMS.